How to Trace a Cold Case

A MAGS AND BIDDY GENEALOGY MYSTERY
BOOK FIVE

ELIZA WATSON

ISBN-10: 1-950786-11-0 (ebook)

ISBN-13: 978-1-950786-11-4 (ebook)

ISBN-13: 978-1-950786-12-1 (paperback)

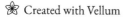 Created with Vellum

Books by Eliza Watson

NONFICTION
Genealogy Tips & Quips

FICTION

A Mags and Biddy Genealogy Mystery Series

How to Fake an Irish Wake (Book 1)

How to Snare a Dodgy Heir (Book 2)

How to Handle an Ancestry Scandal (Book 3)

How to Spot a Murder Plot (Book 4)

How to Trace a Cold Case (Book 5)

The Travel Mishaps of Caity Shaw Series

Flying by the Seat of My Knickers (Book 1)

Up the Seine Without a Paddle (Book 2)

My Christmas Goose Is Almost Cooked (Book 3)

My Wanderlust Bites the Dust (Book 4)

Live to Fly Another Day (Book 5)

When in Doubt Don't Chicken Out (Book 6)

For additional books by Eliza Watson visit
www.elizawatson.com.

Dear Reader,

Did you know that Halloween's origins date back over 2,000 years to Ireland's ancient Samhain festival? The pagan religious festival marked the end of summer and the beginning of the Celtic new year. Samhain is pronounced SAH-win, not Sam-hane. My sister Sandra and I learned the correct pronunciation when attending the Samhain Festival of Fire on the Hill of Ward in Athboy, County Meath. Many people believe the festival originated here in Ireland's Midlands.

During that Halloween trip, we also visited several castles. We received a private tour of Leap Castle, often referred to as the most haunted castle in the world. And Charleville Castle, which appeared on the TV shows *Scariest Places on Earth* and *Ghost Hunters International*. We didn't encounter any ghosts, but we freaked ourselves out several times. The haunted locations inspired the estate setting in *How to Trace a Cold Case* where Mags and Biddy uncover a buried skeleton. Let the Halloween shenanigans begin!

At the end of this story, I've included two research articles from my nonfiction book, *Genealogy Tips & Quips*: "Psst. Did You Hear About... A Newspaper's Gossip Column Might Provide Some Juicy Family History" and "Playing a Genealogist Sleuth: Inspector Clouseau or Sherlock Holmes?" I hope my tips inspire you to begin tracing your family tree or help you break down a brick wall!

Cheers!
Eliza Watson

To my husband, Mark.
Thank you for always making our Ireland trips
absolutely brilliant.

One

GALE-FORCE WINDS HOWLED through the massive oaks outside, rattling the old stately home. Rain lashed against the weathered windows as if determined to break in and whisk away the library's musty smell and clean the scarred wooden floors. My best friend, Biddy McCarthy, stood next to me, paralyzed with fear. She was on the verge of fainting from stage fright rather than from hanging out at a haunted house on Halloween night. Whereas I was about to pass out because my Queen Victoria costume was too tight!

Biddy stared directly at the television camera. This would likely end her constant bragging about having "starred" in two episodes of Ireland's *Rags to Riches Roadshow*. Currently, during the show's first live filming, I was reading or skipping over everyone's lines—which I'd written—scrolling on the teleprompter. At least my recently discovered cousins, Simon and Michelle, had excuses for not reading theirs. Simon's flight from England had been canceled. A flooded motorway in Northern Ireland prevented Michelle from driving down to Kilcarrigy, County Westmeath. The wicked storm hadn't been due to hit here until tomorrow.

Appropriate weather for the morbid Halloween episode. "Mourning Jewelry and Heirlooms: Commemorating the Dead and Uniting the Living."

The show's antique book appraiser, Kiernan Moffat, slipped the pipe from his mouth, part of his Sherlock Holmes costume. The scent of the man's signature spearmint gum filled the air, though, and not the woodsy smell of tobacco. Kiernan was flying solo as the host since his friend, the mourning jewelry expert, hadn't made it over from Dublin. Following our introduction, he was now providing viewers with a bit of background on Victorian mourning jewelry. Prior to our segment, a woman with a valuable pre-Victorian mourning ring was attempting to locate possible relations with an identical ring. Something similar had happened with me. Thanks to my family locket, I'd found cousins and traced my Fitzsimmons line.

The appraiser was about to segue into my story. I jabbed Biddy with my elbow. Her gaze still frozen on the camera, she managed a faint smile. Jane Austen would roll over in her grave if she saw Biddy dressed as the author's brave and assertive fictional character Elizabeth Bennet in *Pride and Prejudice*.

Kiernan Moffat's blue-eyed gaze narrowed with interest behind his wire glasses, studying my necklace. "After Mags's family locket was stolen from her home, she happened upon the dead thief with a mysterious purple pouch when visiting her grandparents' graves. Turned out it contained her locket and the remains of an unknown relative." He arched an intrigued brow.

Biddy nodded. "Thanks to my cousin—"

I nudged my friend, who stopped reading my lines.

Biddy bit down on her lower lip, muffling a distressed squeak.

"Yes, thanks to a newfound cousin of mine, I learned that the locket once displayed a vintage photo of our ancestor at her funeral." I placed a hand on the heart-shaped gold locket and a small key on a chain around my neck. "It also contained a woven lock of the woman's silver hair behind beveled glass."

The young cameraman shuddered, and the producer, a middle-age blond woman, grimaced.

"It might seem a bit creepy, but I'm thankful to have a photo of my two-time great-grandmother. Dead or alive. Piecing together clues from the locket enabled me to solve my family mystery and identify the remains in the pouch as those of my grandfather's sister. My ancestor's initials were engraved on the front of the locket, and the jeweler's logo inside it. This, along with genealogy research, allowed me to trace our family from Birmingham to Scotland to Northern Ireland, then finally to Ireland."

I turned to the appraiser. "Luckily, you recalled having met a woman wearing an identical locket, which led me to my second cousin, Michelle Thompson, in County Down." I'd promised to give my absent cousin credit for helping me trace our family line. "I'd never even heard of mourning jewelry. You set me off on the exciting journey of uncovering the secret of my grandpa Fitzsimmons's family. A past that led me to discovering a distant connection to Ireland's famous hero Michael Collins."

And a family of borderline felons. In all fairness to my

great-grandfather—who'd broken into his grandfather's home and punched him out—the guy had deserved it. He'd planted false evidence, and my great-grandfather's dad was imprisoned, where he'd perished.

"A simply fascinating story." The appraiser slipped the pipe back between his lips as if pondering the outcome of a puzzling mystery. The antique book appraiser had inherited the entire first-edition Sherlock Holmes series and hundreds of books lining the library's wooden shelves behind us, along with a share in this estate, from his grandmother. The vintage books were featured in the opening segment of the show.

A loud bang sounded against a red-draped window, startling us. I expected shards of shattered glass to come flying across the room and stab someone. A crew member raced to the window to make sure the satellite dish and tall telescoping mast hadn't blown over with the broadcasting van. It was a miracle that the show was still transmitting. Perhaps the surrounding woods were providing a buffer of sorts.

"It appears someone or some*thing* is dying to get in through the window." Kiernan flashed viewers a mysterious smile.

Gale-force winds often washed out roads, downed electrical wires, and destroyed fairy gardens. When I was ten, Grandma Fitzsimmons and I had made a garden under the ash tree in what was now my backyard, having inherited her home. A massive windstorm had swept the fairies and their homes off to a neighbor's field, except for a tiny red door nailed to the base of the tree. The door hid a secret space for leaving the fairies notes, wishes, or gifts.

"Queen Victoria made mourning jewelry en vogue after the death of her husband, Albert," I said. "She wore his photo in a locket for forty years and nothing but black until her death." I swept a hand down the front of my velvet gown —a plaid design in green, blue, red, black, and white. "This Clan MacDonnell of Glengarry tartan dress is a replica of the one worn by Princess Victoria of Kent shortly before she became queen." The fancy gown had a full pleated skirt, small matching bows down the front of its tight-fighting V-waist bodice, a scooped neckline trimmed with lace, and puffy elbow-length sleeves with ribbons. "Queen Victoria, Prince Albert, and their children often wore Scottish tartan fabrics, making them even more popular in the nineteenth century." I paused for a breather, making sure I didn't suck in too much air and split a seam on the bodice. "Speaking of Scotland, I recently stayed at Dalwade Castle Hotel and Spa. A lovely place outside of Edinburgh where the queen and her husband were once guests."

The appraiser's blue eyes dimmed with disapproval, yet his smile remained.

If the guy hadn't immediately brushed off my suggestion of filming a future episode at the medieval castle, I wouldn't have had to resort to such blatant promo. And likely wouldn't have paid a Scottish seamstress a crazy amount for the dress. But this was my one shot at introducing millions of viewers to the castle hotel. I had a personal interest in the place staying afloat. Last month, while attending a Murray family reunion there with Dad and Biddy, I discovered the identity of my biological father, Ian Murray, Dad's second cousin. Dad and several Murray relations were investing in the castle's refurbishments, and I was leading the hotel's cemetery restoration project. I wasn't about to let down my family.

I provided viewers with a bit more background on my locket journey before Kiernan directed attention to a framed war medal on an antique table next to us.

"Sadly, I'm not aware of any mourning jewelry in my family. However, I have this precious war medal that enabled my dear Irish grandmother to properly *mourn* my Scottish grandfather, who died in World Word Two."

A ferocious gust of wind pelleted rain against the windows, rattling the glass. An antique watercolor painting dropped from the faded green wall and crashed onto the wooden floor. Objects clattered against shelves and tables. The set lights and candelabra chandelier above us flickered.

The room went dark.

My heart raced, and Biddy squeezed my arm.

"Why isn't the generator kicking in?" Kiernan demanded.

"Not sure," the set manager yelled out. "Checking on it."

"I have a torch...somewhere." The producer's frantic voice was followed by sounds of her rifling through a bag.

Moments later, the lights flashed back on.

I blinked in surprise at the empty table.

"What the bloody..." the appraiser muttered.

His grandfather's treasured military medal was gone.

The man's gaze darted to the camera. "Go to commercial."

Biddy let out a relieved rush of air. "Finally."

I unzipped the back of my dress partway, taking a deep breath, not feeling nearly as relieved as Biddy.

I had no time to be solving a mystery!

Kiernan's gaze darted around at the half dozen crew members and Biddy and me. "Whoever nicked my grandfather's medal had best return it immediately. Your Halloween shenanigans are in very poor taste."

Everyone looked at each other, nobody taking responsibility for having swiped the medal.

"I can't believe I just made a total eejit out of myself in front of the entire world," Biddy whined, carrying on like the drama queen Lydia Bennet, more so than her sensible sister Lizzie.

Kiernan shot Biddy an incredulous look. "This isn't the time to go on about acting like a complete gobshite on live TV."

Bottom lip trembling, Biddy fought back tears and dropped down into a brown leather wingback chair with a thud.

Poor Biddy. Her hairstylist mom had spent hours on her elaborate blond updo adorned with delicate strings of pearls. It resembled the actress Keira Knightley's when Lizzie had attended Mr. Bingley's ball. Biddy's costume also included a cream-colored Regency empire dress with a cream satin ribbon around the waist.

The appraiser's gaze darkened. "I demand whoever took the medal put it back now. Even if your intention was to add a bit of Halloween intrigue to a haunted setting hoping to boost ratings, it was a wretched plan."

The producer pointed a stern finger at Kiernan. "That's something *you* would do, not us, isn't it now?"

True.

Kiernan sneered at the woman.

The cameraman held up a halting hand. "We're on in five..."

Biddy sprang from the chair and joined us.

"You should sit this next part out," I told her.

"I need to redeem myself or everyone will think I'm totally daft. I'm fine."

No time to argue, I shoved aside my frustration rather than Biddy and smiled at the camera as we returned to live TV.

"Where are all my lines?" Biddy whispered, staring at the teleprompter's dark screen.

The device hadn't come back on with the rest of the equipment. She hadn't memorized her lines as I'd requested, so I discreetly pushed Biddy from in front of the camera.

"A bit of a filming glitch from the brutal storm, not the resident ghost. Or was it?" Kiernan flashed viewers a mysterious grin, back on track.

The appraiser was a smooth talker. A skill that had undoubtedly kept the unscrupulous man out of prison.

With great pride, he discussed the medal without directing attention to the empty table. How his Scottish grandfather had earned the medal for saving the lives of numerous men before he'd fallen victim to enemy fire. How the wealthy owner of this stately home, Ernest Dunphy, had married Kiernan's widowed grandmother and taken in her and her three children, including Kiernan's father. At the end, I encouraged viewers to dig out their heirlooms and see if one might help them piece together a century-old family mystery. Also, to check out my website for further details on my mourning jewelry story and genealogy services.

The credits started rolling.

Biddy let out a whimper. "Everyone is at my parents' pub watching the show, including Collin, who won't be wanting to date a complete muppet."

Kiernan rolled his eyes. "Enough with the drama." His gaze darted around at his coworkers. "If everyone continues to deny this was some sort of misguided prank, that means one of you nicked my grandfather's medal with an ulterior motive."

Cowriter Mags Murray.

I smiled proudly at my name on the screen for the entire world to see.

Kiernan's darkened gaze shot from person to person. "I insist that everyone be frisked."

"Mad, are ya?" Biddy shrieked. "I won't be stripping to prove I didn't nick the bloody yoke."

I gestured to my tartan-patterned gown. "Believe me, before I unzipped this, I couldn't even have slipped a piece of paper between me and the thing."

Kiernan turned to the producer, quirking a suspicious brow.

The woman swept a hand down the front of her pocketless black dress. "Where would I have hidden it? If you didn't hide it to boost ratings, you nicked it for the insurance money."

That was certainly plausible. Biddy and I'd first encountered the shifty appraiser when searching for a stolen unpublished manuscript involving the famous author Brendan Quigley. We'd witnessed Kiernan's clandestine meeting at a Dublin hotel, offering a university professor a deal on the stolen manuscript. Then he gave the rightful owner, Aidan Neil, the name of a forger to complete the book in exchange for a percentage of the manuscript's sale. The appraiser likely had been flying just far enough under the authority's radar for years to not have been caught.

"Have you gone absolutely mad?" Kiernan threw his arms up in the air. "Go ahead. Frisk me."

"It's your family's home," the producer spat. "You'd know of any secret hiding spots." Her gaze narrowed on Kiernan's brown shoes and the surrounding wood floor. "Why did you insist on standing in that exact spot when I'd recommended filming over there?"

The lighting guy nodded. "And the antique desk in front of the bookcase would have made a brilliant backdrop."

The producer marched over to Kiernan and stomped her black heel on the floorboards. "Bet there's a loose board ya could have easily lifted to stash the medal with no one knowing."

Kiernan looked appalled.

However, I swore I heard a hollow echo under a board she was stomping on.

"As if I would hide a precious family heirloom under the floor with rodents and who knows what. I will not stand here and be accused of such a thing."

"Then move so I can be checking the floorboards beneath your feet," she snapped.

The security guard rushed into the room. The large man's panicked gaze darted around. "Everything okay, is it? Could hear ya all the way down at the entrance."

"Maybe you should have checked on us when the lights went out and my grandfather's war medal went missing."

The guard wore a baffled expression. "When did the electricity be going out? Wasn't out downstairs."

A chill raced through me.

"Talking about the medal in the hall, are ya?" he asked.

Everyone bolted out to the hallway to find the framed medal on an antique credenza.

"What the... How did it..." Kiernan snatched up his sacred family heirloom, nervously chewing his gum.

"Janey," Biddy muttered. "Your resident ghost..."

Nobody had left the room. The lights hadn't even been off for a minute. When they'd come back on, everyone was in their same spots, except the producer who had been rifling through gear to find a flashlight. With security at the front door, it would have been difficult for a thief to have snuck inside the house. Now, one could certainly have waltzed out the unsecured front entrance. The filming location hadn't been disclosed until the episode had gone live to prevent such Halloween shenanigans. And what thief would have left behind the stolen item?

Kiernan eyed the producer. "You owe me an apology."

"Whatever for? You're still somehow responsible."

"He was standing next to me the entire time the lights were out," I assured her. "I'd have known if he'd dashed out into the hallway and returned."

"A good thing it wasn't a theft anyway," the guard said. "The dirt drive is nearly washed out. Gardai wouldn't have been making their way down it. And don't have mobile service to be ringing 'em either."

Panic seized Biddy's face. "How are we going to get out of here?"

The guy shrugged, making me feel far from safe and secure.

"I'll walk the thirty-some kilometers home if I have to!" Biddy shrieked.

I'd happily walk the distance, thankful there was no mystery to solve. I would arrive home just in time to find dozens of emails from potential clients sitting in my inbox.

However, the hairs prickling the back of my neck dampened my optimism.

Two

THE CREW WAS BARELY SPEAKING to each other, let alone to Kiernan, as they packed up their equipment and gear. The appraiser watched his coworkers like a hawk so they couldn't snatch a rare book, his vintage humidor containing Cuban cigars at a hundred euros each, or other valuable antiques. He also made sure nobody dared to step a muddy foot in the library. Everyone had been directed to stage all equipment in the large entry foyer before loading the vehicles. Hopefully, the work truck and vans made it down the nearly flooded drive. If we all had to stay the night, someone might not make it out alive.

The appraiser shrugged off his brown cape trench coat and draped it over the back of the leather desk chair. He headed over to a beverage cart, poured a whiskey from a crystal decanter, and took a swig of the amber-colored liquor. "I can't believe everyone suspected me of nicking a treasured family heirloom merely to increase ratings."

Biddy's gaze narrowed with curiosity. "What about *other* families' heirlooms?"

I shot her a cautioning glance, even though the appraiser knew I suspected his involvement in dodgy dealings. Upon discovering felons in my Fitzsimmons family line, I'd decided against moving forward with this episode. When Kiernan threatened to film it regardless, I'd threatened to go to the authorities. About what, I wasn't certain. Everything I had against the guy was pure speculation. In the end, I'd reconsidered and agreed to appear on the show. After all, my family story demonstrated that, good or bad, you needed to pursue the truth. What you thought was bad might turn out good.

He sneered at Biddy. "Suddenly you're Chatty Cathy after standing there like a zombie the entire filming."

"Not the *entire* filming," she snapped.

Yeah, she'd opened her mouth once to read *my* lines.

"You've certainly seemed to have ticked off a few coworkers." I glanced over at the producer glaring at Kiernan while she packed a bag.

"The woman can't let it go. I should know better than to get involved with a coworker. She's likely in on it with that gobshite who once stepped in for me when I fell ill. He's been trying to get me sacked ever since. Hasn't a clue about rare and vintage books. The idiot thought Leo Tolstoy wrote *Dr. Zhivago.*"

Biddy and I exchanged questioning glances.

He let out an exasperated groan. "Boris Pasternak was the author." The appraiser slipped the book off a shelf and handed me the thick hardcover. He peered over at Biddy. "At least watch the movie. It's a classic."

Biddy jutted out her chin. "As if I can't read."

Kiernan ignored her reaction, brushing a finger across the spines of cloth and leather book covers, leaving a dust-free trail behind. "I've read every book in this library. Some at a much younger age than my grandmother approved of. First editions and rare books are at my home in Cork to best be preserved. Yet it wouldn't seem right to empty all these shelves. I couldn't bear to walk into a library void of books."

Hundreds of books lined the wooden shelves. I hadn't read this many books in my life, including school textbooks and Little Golden Books as a child. Not even if I counted having read my favorite, *The Poky Little Puppy*, a hundred times.

Wearing a reminiscent look, Kiernan placed a hand on the brown leather desk chair. "Ernest would sit here and work while I curled up in that chair next to the window, reading for hours. Don't know what my grandmother would have done if he hadn't taken her and her children in after her husband was killed in the war."

I'd never seen the man so sentimental about antiques. He appeared to hold a deep respect for his family heirlooms, but as Biddy had asked, did that mean he held the same respect for *other* people's?

"Despite my siblings not having appreciated the home's heritage, our father placed it in a family trust. I bought out their shares when they wanted to sell the place. While growing up, they preferred to revel in wild tales of hauntings. They'd have friends over and stay up all night waiting for ghosts to materialize. My older brother once went so far as to fabricate a haunting, playing mysterious tape-recorded noises in the attic. They'd have been scared out of their wits if they'd ever truly experienced paranormal activity, such as I have."

Biddy's eyes widened in awe. "An actual haunting?"

He nodded. "I'd often hear muffled voices and faint

music coming from somewhere in the house at precisely midnight. Dear Ernest passed away here nearly forty years ago. Thought it would be a nice tribute to film at the estate."

Biddy shuddered.

"And my therapist recommended I face my fears."

"I'm sure there's a logical explanation for the hauntings," I said. "And tonight's theft was undoubtedly connected to one of your coworkers."

"Or a spiteful family member jealous that I'd inherited the medal. However, I know for a fact they're in Australia."

"The person could have been hiding in the hallway waiting for the lights to go off so he could sneak in and swipe the medal," Biddy said. "Or was hiding in a secret passageway. Then snuck out into the hallway while we were busy filming."

Kiernan laughed. "Quite the imagination. There aren't any secret passageways or hidden rooms in this house. I'd have known if such a thing existed."

"Are you sure?" I asked. "I swear I heard a hollow echo when the producer was stomping her foot on the floorboards."

"Yes, I'm quite certain." Kiernan's suspicious gaze narrowed on the cameraman zipping up the last bag. The guy slung it over his shoulder and walked out. "I'll be right back." The appraiser flew out the door after the potential thief.

I set the hardcover book on the desk, planning to accidentally leave it behind. I needed to read more. However, I doubted the literary classic would inspire me to *keep* reading.

"It wasn't merely my imagination," I told Biddy and then knelt where Kiernan had been standing. I rapped my knuckles against several boards until I heard the hollow sound. Biddy and I gasped with excitement.

My heart raced. "I bet it's a priest hole."

"A what?"

"During the English Reformation and under penal laws in Ireland, being a Catholic priest was a punishable crime. So Catholic nobility and the upper class began building priest hiding spots in their fireplaces, attics, staircases, and under floors."

Biddy frowned, disappointed at the prospect of a boring historical find. "Maybe it's hidden cash or valuables."

"What are you doing?" Kiernan entered and eyed us kneeling on the floor. "Please leave. I'd like to forget about the show's first and undoubtedly last live episode."

I gave the floorboard another rap. "Can't you hear that hollow sound?"

"Honestly, right now, I don't care if the bloody crown jewels are buried under there. I'm wrecked."

Fine. I stood and brushed the dust from my dress. "Outside of the trick someone played on you, I think tonight went well. The show mysteriously cutting out undoubtedly piqued viewers' interest."

He tilted his head to the side, massaging his neck. "Yes, I suppose the roof could have blown down to Offaly or a tree fallen through a window."

"Or your medal could have actually been nicked," Biddy said.

His shoulders relaxed. "The others made it down the drive. You'll be grand."

"They also have a truck and vans." Biddy grabbed our purses from a desk drawer. "But no worries. This is the last place I'd want to spend the night. If anyone should want to erase this evening from their memory, it's me."

"Cheers." Kiernan topped off his drink.

Biddy and I sashayed into the hallway, our long dresses sweeping against the wood floor, sending dust bunnies hopping. We hiked up our skirts before heading down the open staircase so we didn't stumble and fall to the bottom, our bloody bodies landing on the antique Persian rug no longer protected by a drop cloth. The appraiser would be more worried about rushing his precious rug to a cleaner than Biddy and me to the emergency room. I opened the massive front door. The wind seized the wooden door, banging it against the wall. Sheets of rain blew in and drenched us before we'd even stepped outside.

"Lovely," Biddy muttered.

Once again we raised our dress hems, preparing to make our way across the muddy drive to Biddy's small gray car parked under a towering oak tree. Not the best place to have parked during a windstorm. Her night could have gotten even worse if a large branch had taken out the windshield.

"At least Elizabeth Bennet loved traipsing through fields," Biddy said. "Her dresses always had muddy hems."

I struggled against the wind to gain forward momentum. A gust blew my wet hair from its bun and slapped clumps against my cheeks and in my eyes. Mud squished inside my black flats. We finally reached the car and flew inside as the rain diminished to an annoying drizzle. I dropped back against the seat, letting out a whoosh of air. We whipped off our shoes and blew through a packet of wipes from the glove compartment cleaning off our feet. Biddy caught her breath and went to pull out. The tires spun in the mud, making a horrific noise.

"Are ya bloody serious?" Biddy smacked her palm against the steering wheel. She pressed down on the accelerator, and more tire spinning.

I groaned in misery. "I'll give you a push."

Cussing up a storm, I shoved my clean feet into the muddy flats and trudged to the back of the car. The vehicle was small, but I lacked upper-body strength and was weighed down by an elaborate gown. I braced my hands against the trunk and gave it my all. The spinning tires splattered mud over my dress's skirt, which fueled my anger and adrenaline. The car went deeper into the mud. After several failed attempts, I rested my butt against the car's back end. My foot slipped out from under me and sank into the mud. It reappeared with a small tree branch on top of it. I braced a hand against the car and grabbed the branch with the other. I went to toss it aside and discovered it was attached to several other small...*bones.*

I gasped in horror and dropped the skeletal remains.

Unlike many Irish homes, the estate's grounds and the house's exterior hadn't been decorated for Halloween. Prior to the storm, no skeleton had been hanging from the tree or displayed in a coffin propped up against the large trunk.

"Are you even pushing?" Biddy yelled out the car window.

"Get back here! And bring a flashlight!"

"How am I supposed to drive if I'm helping you push?"

"Now!" I grabbed a handful of leaves from the ground and scrubbed my foot, attempting to remove any skeletal residue.

The car door slammed shut, and Biddy plodded back. Blinded by the flashlight's yellow beam, I directed it from my face and toward the ground.

Biddy sucked in some serious air. "What the..." She leaned down for a closer look, sweeping her hair back off her face. "Is that a skeleton's foot, is it?"

I nodded, shuddering. "And it's attached to a leg. Is it an animal's or a human's?"

"Janey," she muttered. "Human would be my guess."

"Is it real?"

"Haven't a clue."

"You must have seen real skeletons in nursing school."

"Not much a nurse could be doing to save a skeleton. A person is beyond saving at that point. We used fake ones. This one doesn't appear fake. Why would a fake skeleton be buried in the yard?"

"Why would a *real* one be buried in the yard?" I shrieked.

Biddy nodded. "True. The only real skeleton I've ever seen was one Halloween, when my uncle Seamus and his undertaker friend had one in a casket in the back of a hearse. Were charging people a pint for a snap with it."

"That's disgusting."

"In all fairness to Seamus, he'd assumed the yoke was fake. I mean, where would his friend have gotten a real one?"

"Gee, where would an undertaker get a skeleton?"

"An *undertaker*, not a grave robber. Anyway, the fella's friend was building a conservatory when he came across it. After Halloween, they contacted the garda. It turned out to be hundreds of years old."

"We definitely need to contact the garda. Or rather, Kiernan needs to."

Biddy grasped my arm. "What if he's the one who buried the body? We'll be next to keep us quiet."

We pondered the likelihood of the pompous appraiser burying a body on his family's estate. I tried to envision the man breaking a sweat while shoveling up heavy loads of earth so he could heave a body into an open grave, dirt ruining his manicured nails and designer clothing.

I shook my head. "I think he sticks to white-collar crime. I don't see him offing someone."

Biddy nodded. "He'd flip out if he got a spot of blood on his Italian leather shoes." Her gaze narrowed. "He could always have hired a hit man. Maybe someone was planning on ratting him out for one of his scams."

Besides me, who'd have been stupid enough to threaten the sketchy man?

"For what a hit man charges, I don't think he'd be leaving the body on his client's property. I just don't see Kiernan involved with a murder, period."

Biddy didn't look convinced. "I suppose even dodgy blokes might have standards."

We trudged back across the muddy drive. Blown to bits and sopping wet, we hiked up the stairs to the library, where classical music played. Kiernan was relaxing in a leather wing-back chair next to a roaring fire, eyes closed, cheeks rosy. A crystal glass in his hand.

Biddy swept her wet hair back from her face. "Great news. Think we figured out who's haunting your house."

The man's eyes shot open. His horrified gaze narrowed on our soaked dresses forming puddles on the wood floor. "I couldn't care less if you saw the ghost of bloody Queen Victoria."

"Oh, I think you'll care about this," I said.

He sprang from the chair. "You walked across my custom-made rug like"—he gestured a flustered hand at our drenched outfits—"that? After I removed the drop cloth? And then you walked up the staircase?"

"Well, we didn't leap across your Persian rug, then slide *up* the banister," I quipped.

"It's *Turkish*." He polished off his drink. "Will this bloody night ever end?"

Biddy and I shook our heads.

He rolled his eyes. "Your car is stuck, isn't it? And you want me to give you a push?"

We shook our heads again.

He quirked a confused brow. "Then why are you still here?"

"A better question would be, why is there a skeleton buried under the tree behind Biddy's car?"

Another exasperated eye roll. "It's undoubtedly a tree limb or a bone the neighbor's dog buried."

Biddy let out an impatient groan. "Mags should be wearing your Sherlock Holmes costume, and you should be dressed like a queen. As a nurse, I guarantee it's a skeleton."

Panic flashed in the man's blue eyes. "If this is more Halloween shenanigans..."

Biddy slapped her fists on her hips. "You think we'd rather be stuck here playing some stupid trick on you than getting ossified at my family's pub after the night I've had? Even a massive dry-cleaning bill won't get the mud out of this stupid dress. I'm going to end up having to buy it just so I can turn around and burn it!"

For what mine had cost, I'd planned on wearing the gown for my wedding, if I ever had one. Hopefully, the ruined dress didn't foreshadow my doomed love life.

Appearing more freaked out by Biddy's meltdown than a possible skeleton in the yard, Kiernan grabbed the caped trench coat from the chair.

"Unless, of course, I can be expensing the cleaner's bill." Biddy stared expectantly at the man.

Kiernan's forehead wrinkled. "To the show?"

"Who else?"

He stalked out of the room and down the staircase, livid over the wet, muddy steps. The filthy *Turkish* rug about sent him over the edge. He exchanged his brown designer shoes for a pair of green wellies by the door. He wisely decided against an umbrella hanging on the coat rack. He flipped on the house's corner security light nearest the tree and Biddy's car. The three of us trudged across the muddy drive. I shined the flashlight on the ground behind the car.

"Jaysus," Kiernan muttered, staring at the skeleton's foot and leg now cleaned off from the rain. He snatched the flashlight from my hand and swept the yellow beam around the yard and into the scary woods beyond. "Come out this instant, whoever you are."

Thankfully, nobody materialized from the creepy trees.

Appearing unnerved, the man vigorously chewed his gum. "It's likely a coworker playing another prank."

"With a *real* skeleton?" Biddy said. "What sicko would do such a thing? In all fairness to my uncle Seamus, he hadn't a clue that skeleton was real."

The appraiser looked at Biddy like she'd gone completely mad. "Fine. I'll deal with it in the morning and make sure it receives a proper burial elsewhere."

"You need to call the garda now," I demanded.

"I'm not turning my family home into a crime scene investigation. Besides, my grandmother's garden shed stood in that exact spot until I had it torn down this past summer. The remains are well over a hundred years old. One more day will not make a difference. They just found some thousand-year-old Viking under a bar down in Cork."

"What if it was your grandmother?" I asked.

His head snapped back in horror. "I assure you my grandmother is buried and resting peacefully at the cemetery up the road. I attended the wake and funeral as a lad."

"I meant it's *someone's* grandparent, or parent, or sibling, or who knows. We owe it to the living and the dead to not only give the person a burial, but an identity." I slipped my phone from my purse even though it didn't have cell service. "I'm calling the garda."

Kiernan pushed the phone away from my ear. He checked the Rolex on his wrist. "It's nearly midnight. You'll merely upset the local guard for getting him out of bed over something that could wait until morning." He eyed his vintage watch. "You're always admiring my watches. Perhaps you'd fancy this one. Would make a lovely gift for your father."

I couldn't help but always notice his watches. He was constantly checking the time, making sure everyone noticed them.

I stared at him in disbelief. "Are you trying to buy us off?"

He raised a brow. "Cash, then?"

"How much?" Biddy asked.

I shot her a disapproving glance.

"Was merely curious what he'd be paying..."

"I'm not leaving until the garda arrive," I said. "If I can't call them from here, then I'll hike to the nearest house and call. Before you know it, the entire town will be popping by to see—"

"Fine." Kiernan yanked down his coat sleeve, covering the watch. "You can ring them from the house phone."

Sadly, the prickly hairs on the back of my neck were right as usual. So much for a restful night's sleep.

An hour later, Kiernan, Biddy, and I peered out the library's window down at several gardai in yellow reflective vests and the forensic team resembling ghostly figures in their white coveralls. Two gardai struggled to hold the portable lighting in place. A gust of wind whisked the blue-and-white crime scene tape up toward the dark clouds.

The team had confirmed the remains were human. The state pathologist and anthropologist were heading over from Dublin on the partially washed-out motorway. They'd determine if the skeletal remains became part of a police investigation or an anthropological study. Thankfully, Biddy and I didn't need to stick around. We'd given our statements to an officer, who was giving us a ride home. Biddy's car was being held at the scene until it could be confirmed that no skeletal remains or other evidence had become lodged in the vehicle's undercarriage.

Biddy was freaked out over the idea of a bone one day dropping out from underneath her car. She was also upset about her car being detained because she was working the early shift at the hospital's pediatric ward.

Kiernan was in shock, resembling Biddy's earlier zombie state in front of the camera. Biddy and I had spread the drop cloth back over the Turkish rug and unrolled a narrow sheet of plastic across the library's wood floor before the officers had arrived.

The appraiser braced a hand on the back of a large brown leather chair. "I used to sit right here by the window absorbed in books for hours, occasionally peering out at my grandmother's gardening shed and the woman tending to her lovely flowers. Having been clueless about what lie under the innocent shed."

Had his grandmother been clueless?

"Are you sure the shed was built before Ernest Dunphy's time?" Biddy asked.

"Yes, I'm sure," he snapped. "It was most certainly built in the mid-eighteen hundreds, same as the house and other outbuildings."

"The body could easily have been buried after the structure was built," Biddy said.

"If you're insinuating that my grandmother and Ernest had known about what was under the shed, absolutely not. She'd once come across a bird carcass among her flower seeds and nearly fainted, refusing to enter the shed until the yoke was removed. She certainly wouldn't have gone near the building if she'd realized a skeleton was buried beneath it."

Perhaps her husband, Ernest, hadn't told her. One of many secrets the man might have kept from his wife.

Three

"YOU'RE NOT MOVING IN HERE." I eyed Biddy curled up in a green fleece blanket on my living room couch.

She snuggled into the overstuffed red cushions. "Just for a few days...or weeks. Until the hype dies down from the show and everyone forgets what an eejit I made of myself."

That would take *years*. Locals knew everything and forgot nothing. Now, months after I'd found a dead man on my grandparents' graves, I was still often greeted as the Tombstone Terminator or Shovel Slayer at McCarthy's pub. The nicknames had circulated along with rumors that I'd killed the man with his shovel when catching him digging up the graves. However, in Biddy's case it wasn't merely a handful of locals, but millions of viewers worldwide had witnessed her embarrassment.

"Thought I had to drive you to work in an hour?" I popped several roasted pumpkin seeds into my mouth. I'd cleaned out the insides of a half dozen pumpkins on my front stoop. While growing up, every Halloween I looked forward to Mom's salty treat.

"Called in sick," Biddy said.

"How can you afford to call in sick?"

"How can I afford *not* to?" Biddy buried her face in a floral throw pillow and groaned.

This past spring Nurse Biddy had *temporarily* cut back to three days a week at the pediatric ward, after we'd helped recover her now boyfriend Collin Neil's family heirloom. A feature on *Rags to Riches Roadshow* had launched the unpublished novel connected to the famous author Brendan Quigley into a bidding war. Collin's grandmother had insisted I receive a 10 percent cut of the five-hundred-thousand-euro publishing advance. I'd split my share with Biddy, who'd thought she'd won the lottery and cut her hours at work. Yet she lived at home. Becoming roomies would definitely put a major strain on our friendship.

I had to nip this in the bud.

"You know what? That'd actually work great if you moved in."

Her head shot up from the pillow. "Really?"

"Yeah. I could use help with expenses so I can save money for a new conservatory. I'm surprised the roof didn't fly off last night and take out a few of Mattie Nolan's cows. By cutting my bills in half, I could afford to build a new one."

Biddy's smile faded.

I plopped down onto the couch, peering over at the roaring fire in the green cast-iron stove tucked into a brick fireplace. "Peat, wood, and fire starters run a few hundred euros a season. Electricity about seventy-five euros a month but probably closer to a hundred with two of us. Groceries around three hundred euros..."

Biddy's jaw dropped. "A month?"

I nodded. "Food isn't cheap here."

"Because you buy brands from the States, like Froot Loops. Get the store brand."

"Why should Pinky have to suffer because we're roomies? He enjoys his daily Froot Loops." Pinky, a large sheep with a bright-pink splash of dye on his wool, hung out in my yard more than his owner's field. "He helped me get over my fear of sheep. He's earned the name-brand cereal."

"Suppose I could eat meals at my parents."

"You'll be here the rest of the time eating my snacks, drinking my wine, using my toilet paper..." Not much different from how it was now. I let out a disheartened sigh. "You haven't even moved in and we're arguing about cereal and toilet paper."

Biddy's shoulders slumped in defeat, and she dropped back against the couch. "Even though I desperately want to move out of my parents' place and hide out from the world, I have it pretty good there."

"Ya think?" My phone dinged the arrival of a text. My aunt Ava Murray in Scotland.

You two lassies were smashing last night! Lovely tartan gown. Thanks loads for mentioning the castle. Archie was over the moon.

The castle's English owner, Archie McLean, had sent me two emails, ecstatic about the free publicity. Refurbishments were becoming much more costly than expected. Lovely. Nothing like adding a bit more pressure when I delivered the devastating news that the show wouldn't be filming at the castle.

Was a ghost messing with the filming?

I hadn't shared my skeleton discovery with anyone. My

dad would be first on my list. Until a month ago, he'd have been the only one on my list.

Suddenly having an aunt was weird, especially when I'd always believed she was my second cousin once removed. My mom had been an only child, and my dad might as well have been. His brother worked in a remote oil field in Canada, and I'd only seen him a handful of times. Recently I'd spent more time in Scotland with my newly discovered uncle Tavish. I'd also gained a first cousin whose dad, my uncle Malcolm, was murdered at our family reunion. Even weirder than these new close relations was having two dads. I'd received texts from both men last night. Ian had watched the show in Edinburgh, and Dad had caught it live on the BBC in Florida.

Of course, my sisters Mia and Emma hadn't congratulated me on my show's appearance. They hadn't even reached out to me last month after Dad told them about my DNA discovery and biological father. My sisters had stopped speaking to me nearly a year ago when I'd inherited Grandma's house and opted not to sell it and split the money with them.

Biddy snatched her ringing phone from the cocktail table. She glanced at the caller ID, then tossed it onto the other end of the couch. "Collin. If I can't hide out here, how about in a hut on some remote South Pacific island where nobody has a tellie or internet and doesn't know who I am?"

I felt bad for Biddy. If I'd been the one to make a fool of myself on live TV, I'd certainly expect her to be compassionate.

"How about we use the teleprompter as an excuse? We can say it was out our entire segment. And you hadn't memorized all the lines like I had because I'd written them. Even though I'd recommended you learn them."

Biddy perked up on the couch. "That's totally brill. And at least partly true. The yoke was banjaxed after the electricity came back on."

The doorbell rang.

Biddy sprang from the couch, snatching up the blanket. "If it's Collin, I'm sleeping and will be all day." She flew into the master bedroom, where she'd slept.

Nine months after Grandma had been laid out in the bed for her wake, I'd finally replaced the mattress. I still slept in the green guestroom upstairs, where I'd always stayed when visiting Grandma. The room provided a sense of comfort and stability while transitioning into my new life here. For having worked seasonal jobs around the US my entire adult life, I suddenly welcomed a bit of stability.

The doorbell bell rang again and again.

It was likely Gretta Lynch, who'd assisted me with solving several mysteries in the area. I'd expected the older woman to have been camped out on my doorstep last night, wondering why the show had cut out and if there was a mystery involved. Odd that she hadn't even called about it.

I grabbed my long green wool coat from the mudroom's rack and slipped it on over my purple flannel jammies. I peered through the green door's small window at a man in a dark bulky sweatsuit with the hood pulled over his head, hiding his face. A small wreck of a gray car sat in the drive.

"What do you want?" I yelled through the glass.

The guy peeked out from behind the sweatshirt hood.

Kiernan Moffat.

I opened the door, and the appraiser flew inside. He

snapped the blind shut on the mudroom window, the Halloween cling decorations on the glass disappearing. He bolted through the open French doors and closed every blind in the living room. I wasn't sure which was more out of character. The man's sloppy attire or his bizarre behavior.

"What's going on?" I asked.

He slipped the hood from his head, revealing messy dark hair and an unshaven face. "As if you don't know. It's a bloody social media nightmare. Everyone speculating that the skeleton found in my *yard* is from my Moffat family *closet*!"

"As if I had anything to do with it."

"You two were the only ones there outside of the authorities."

"I'm sure your neighbors saw the garda and forensic team vehicles speeding past their houses and down your drive. And like my neighbor Gretta, some people listen to police scanners rather than watch *Law and Order*. The mass media likely caught wind of it same as social media."

Panic flickered in his blue eyes. "That doesn't make me feel better."

"I only have a Facebook account to belong to genealogy groups. Besides, I wouldn't disrespect that person or his loved ones by causing a social media circus. As a genealogist, I have an ethical obligation to help the dead, who can no longer help themselves."

He paced back and forth across the wood floor, nervously chewing his spearmint gum. "I need to hide out."

"Well, you're not staying here. This inn is full." I called out to Biddy on the other side of the bedroom's knotty pine door.

The door opened, and she appeared wrapped in the blanket.

"Do you two also go to the loo together?" he asked.

Biddy's gaze swept the length of the man down to his worn, dirty tennies. "Janey. What happened to you? Been nicking items from the donation bin in the church's lot, have ya?"

Kiernan directed his glare from Biddy to me. "I hadn't intended on staying here." He chewed his gum more vigorously, raking a hand through his hair. "The skeletal remains likely aren't as old as we'd presumed."

"How old are they?" I asked.

He shrugged. "All I know is the remains are those of a human male believed to have been middle age at the time of death. It seems once a person's forty years old it becomes difficult to pinpoint age because of genes, lifestyle, whatever. It's even more difficult to nail down the time since death due to environmental factors. The remains have been taken to Dublin for the state pathologist and anthropologist to exam more closely. I expect further details today, but any testing could take days or weeks. If the death occurred less than seventy years ago, there may be an investigation into the person's identity, or there may not. Depends on the pathologist's and the detective's findings."

"What makes them think the remains may be more recent?" I asked.

"A 1928 pence coin from the Irish Free State was found wedged into the skeleton's joint or...somewhere." He grimaced.

"Janey," Biddy muttered. "Hope that wasn't the fella's lucky penny he carried around in his pants pocket."

I nodded. "No kidding. Although it might prove lucky for him in the end if it helps narrow down his date of death and possibly identify him."

Kiernan's gaze narrowed in concern. "Forget I mentioned that. It isn't public knowledge."

Biddy and I zipped pinched fingers across our lips.

He raised a skeptical brow.

"Could the coin somehow have gotten there another way?" I asked.

He shook his head. "They say not. Either it belonged to the deceased or whoever put him in the ground. Supposedly, the remains were originally several feet under."

"So if it wasn't the victim's coin, it was the killer's..." Biddy mused.

Kiernan's eyes widened. "I never mentioned murder." His voice lowered to a hush, and his gaze darted around at the closed blinds. "Don't be saying *murder* to anyone."

"Who buries a *loved* one under a shed?" Biddy asked.

"I refuse to have the estate involved in a criminal investigation."

"Doubt you'll have a choice," I said.

Biddy tapped a finger against her chin. "Wonder if the murderer is still around."

Kiernan cringed. "Stop saying that word." He heaved a sigh. "The garda promised to share the details with me before releasing them to the public. I might have a ten-minute heads-up so as not to be blindsided by the media."

"Especially if it ends up being a criminal investigation," Biddy said. "Would be nice to know who the person was before the guards do. Be proactive so you can do damage control."

"Why in the world would I need to do damage control? Whoever was under that tree isn't a blood relation of mine. Ernest didn't marry my grandmother until the late 1940s."

"Who's to say the person wasn't buried after that?" Biddy said. "I have twenty-year-old coins in my wallet. Maybe the fella was a coin collector with one from the newly formed Irish Free State era."

Panic flickered in the man's eyes, and he glanced away. "I can't bear the thought of the memory of that fine man, or his family, being tarnished."

"The media won't care if the dead fella isn't actually your relation," Biddy said. "Claiming he's related to a television celebrity would make a post go viral and sell more newspapers than him being related to your step-grandfather, a nobody. Only locals would care about that bit of juicy gossip."

The appraiser sneered at Biddy.

"Sorry, but she's probably right," I said.

Inspiration seized Biddy. "Mags and I could research the person's identity."

"How exactly?" I asked. "Our only clue is a man who died less than ninety-four years ago was buried under the shed. This is a cold case for the garda to solve, not us. Not to mention, I already have a dozen potential new clients and—"

"Thanks to me." Kiernan quirked an intrigued brow. "You're a genealogist. You locate and identify dead people all the time."

"From researching historical records and DNA, not bones. If any of Ernest's relatives are still alive, the garda might do a DNA test and the mystery will be solved."

"That won't identify the person," Biddy said. "We could identify the fella."

The appraiser nodded, warming to the idea.

"As I was saying, besides a long client list, I have to outline Dalwade Castle's cemetery project to help the hotel stay afloat." Hmmm... I eyed the appraiser. "Especially since your show won't be filming there." A sly smile curled my lips.

He shook his head. "Certainly not."

"Why are you so against filming there?" I asked.

"Locations for Scotland's spring itinerary are nearly all determined."

"*Nearly*, so not all," I said.

"That's a totally brill idea." Biddy's face lit up. "Would give me a chance to rebuild my reputation."

The man gave Biddy an incredulous look. "Gone completely mad, have you? Despite this horrific situation, *I* haven't. You won't be appearing in a future episode."

Biddy squared her shoulders. "As if you did so great on your first episode. Surely not."

I felt an ethical obligation to give the skeleton an identity and a proper burial in a family plot if one existed. The poor man deserved to rest in peace since he likely hadn't died in peace. A filming at the castle would be a bonus.

"I think this would be a win-win situation for us both," I said. "If I can identify the skeleton, you agree to film an episode at Dalwade Castle."

Kiernan frowned. "What happened to your ethical obligation to help those who can no longer help themselves?"

"I also need to help *myself* in the process when I can."

"And there's no deal unless I appear on the episode," Biddy said.

I needed to do the show for the castle's sake with or without Biddy.

Kiernan pulled the sweatshirt hood back up over his head and stalked through the mudroom and out the front door.

"Was that a yes or a no?" Biddy asked.

"Think it was a no."

I debated running after him and offering to investigate regardless of Biddy's involvement in the show. Biddy was in a fragile state, yet so was Dalwade Castle. Without sufficient funds, the medieval landmark would fall into disrepair and become one of hundreds of abandoned stately homes and castles that eventually crumbled to the ground.

The doorbell rang.

I hurried through the mudroom and opened the door.

"I'll work on scheduling an episode at your castle in the spring," Kiernan said.

Biddy joined us. "With me."

He shook his head. "That's not a guarantee."

"How about in exchange, I'll be in charge of social media damage control? I have loads of followers, including several celebrities and major businesses."

The lead singer from a local karaoke band wasn't exactly a celebrity. McDonald's had once commented on her praise for Shamrock shakes. And an airline agreed to give her a voucher so she'd stop slamming them on social media about a canceled flight while drowning her sorrows in an airport pub.

Kiernan didn't agree but appeared mildly intrigued by her offer. "Our agreement is based on the castle meeting the show's standards. Either a location scout or I will check out the place."

My heart raced with anticipation. "I need your word that

it'll be a valid reason if you don't select the castle. I'm not doing all the work and then have you back out on the deal."

"Agreed. We can work out the details later."

Not trusting the guy, I jotted down a quick contract on a piece of printer paper. The appraiser signed it, and we shook hands.

"My lawyer will draft up a more official document later today," he said. "You can sign it this evening when you stop by to collect whatever historical records I can locate for the estate and the Dunphys that might assist with identifying the deceased. I know very little about Ernest's family."

I was psyched to once again rap on the library's wooden floorboards, dying to know what might be hidden under them. Curiosity and panic made my heart race. Being in over my head was nothing new. However, the stakes usually weren't as high as helping to save a Scottish castle and keep my family from financial ruin.

Four

"Don't worry—you'll be on the episode," I told Biddy while opening the living room blinds. Fingers crossed *I* was even on the episode, given Kiernan was a shifty character.

Back on the couch, she pulled the blanket up over her head. "Maybe it's best to be leaving those closed."

"I doubt anyone but Collin is looking in people's windows for you. TV viewers have certainly forgotten about you thanks to the skeleton."

Biddy perked up. "True. Things might not be as bad as I feared."

"Except that we haven't a clue how to solve a cold case. And I'm way behind on the cemetery project. I promised Ava and Rhona a progress report within a week, since preparing for the filming has been all consuming. I don't want them to think I'm unreliable."

"You just booked the castle to appear on an episode of *Rags to Riches Roadshow*. It'd cost millions to buy exposure like that. I'd say that's way above and beyond your cemetery project."

"I'm not mentioning it until I'm confident it's a go."

"Besides the show, you kept Ian, Ava's brother and Rhona's lover, from spending life in prison for confessing to a murder he didn't commit. And figured out who *did* kill their brother. You've more than proven yourself worthy and reliable."

I nodded faintly.

"You're so worried what your family thinks about you and helping them out, yet you've hardly had contact with Ian. A bit mad, isn't it?"

If Ian had gone to prison, I'd never have been given a chance to get to know him. Rather than seizing the opportunity, we'd only emailed a few times under the pretense of discussing the castle or my television appearance.

"Let's talk about what a mess I am later. Right now I'm freaking out about the deal I just made with Kiernan Moffat." I massaged my throbbing forehead. "At least with ancestry research I have a starting point with a living person to trace back. Or with a known dead person to trace the tree forward. Even if a Dunphy relation takes a DNA test, I don't think that will determine how the person is related to the deceased—only maybe if it was a close relation, like a parent, sibling, or child."

"The dead fella might not even be a relation of the Dunphys. Could have been some random drifter passing through. Killed in a pub brawl and buried on the grounds when the owners were vacationing in the South of France. Who knows?"

"We need to give the poor guy a name rather than calling him the dead fella, the skeleton…"

"How about Skelly? That's a lovely name for a skeleton. My dad's friend Owen Skelly runs Skelly's pub over in Meath."

"Never heard of that last name before."

"It's scarce."

I nodded. "I like it. Let's go with Skelly."

Biddy's phone dinged. She snatched it up and read the text. "My mum just heard about Skelly from the Guinness fella testing the hoses. She's wondering how we're involved." Biddy glanced up from her phone. "Why does she assume every time there's a dead body or crime within a half hour of Ballycaffey that we're involved?"

"Because we usually are." I flopped down onto the couch. "They say like sixty percent of the time a murder victim knew his killer. That'd mean either a relative or acquaintance of the Dunphy family if they were involved."

"Or a murder occurred during a robbery at their home. The other forty percent of the time the victim is likely killed during a felony of some sort."

"Let's start out optimistic and hope Skelly was connected to the Dunphys. Like an annoying second cousin who dropped by unexpectedly for a visit and never left, then ended up under the shed."

Biddy's gaze narrowed. "Hmm... I don't picture a man named Skelly as being annoying. More of a fun-loving kind of fella."

"We aren't profiling the guy based on his name actually having been Skelly."

"Fine. I was just trying to remain optimistic like you insisted."

The doorbell rang.

I dropped my head back, groaning over another interruption.

"Unless that's my mum, I'm not here." Biddy flew toward the bedroom. "Even if it is her, I'm not." She shut the door.

I went to the mudroom to find my friends Edmond and Rosie smiling anxiously at me through the door's window. Apparently they'd heard about Skelly. I invited the older couple inside. A tall man with unruly gray hair, Edmond slipped off his navy wool coat. He had on slightly wrinkled blue slacks and a white button-up shirt, whereas Rosie wore a crisply pressed royal-blue dress, pink blush on her porcelain cheeks, and perfectly coifed short white hair. As usual, I felt underdressed around the woman, who was always put together. I slipped off my long wool coat and draped it over the back of the love seat.

"It's Rosie and Edmond," I called out to Biddy.

Biddy flung the bedroom door open and shot me an annoyed look for outing her. The couple were the perfect people for her to practice on. They wouldn't be judgmental or taunt her with nicknames like Dizzy Lizzie Bennet. Come to think of it, my nickname Shovel Slayer had been thanks to Biddy.

"We just heard about the skeleton discovered at the show's location last evening," Edmond said. "There when it happened, were ya?"

I nodded. "Right there actually." The couple sat on the edge of the couch cushions as I recounted the shocking events of the previous night.

Rosie shook her head in awe. "How exciting. To find a real skeleton on Halloween of all days. Must say, not a bit surprised it was buried on that dodgy appraiser's property."

Rosie was aware of Biddy and my dealings with the sketchy Kiernan Moffat. Her brother Albert, an antique dealer, also had a poor opinion of the appraiser. I considered Albert a reliable resource for pegging dodgy people. A few years back the man was brought up on charges for buying and selling valuable antiques without provenance—ownership and history records used to authenticate an antique. And his son was currently in prison for insurance fraud.

"In all fairness to the fella," Biddy said, "the remains are likely from before his grandmother married into the family."

I shrugged. "Maybe, maybe not."

Rosie looked skeptical. "Well, before we discuss that, I want to say how lovely you lasses were on the tellie last night. Those costumes were brilliant."

Edmond smiled. "Indeed." He glanced over at Biddy. "Was surprised to have only seen you during the introduction and then for a short bit later. Had expected you on the entire segment."

Biddy and I exchanged surprised glances and relieved smiles. Kudos to the cameraman for successfully cutting Biddy out of the filming.

"I wasn't feeling quite right," Biddy said.

"Ah, luv," Rosie said. "What a pity. There's always next time."

"Right, then," Edmond said. "Thought the tellie was banjaxed when it went dark. Was on my way over to give it a rap when it flashed back on."

Rosie's blue eyes lit with curiosity. "The resident ghost partaking in a few shenanigans, was it?"

"A coworker's shenanigans more likely," I said.

Biddy looked doubtful, holding out for a ghost.

"Such mystery and intrigue for an antique show," Rosie said. "The ratings will surely soar. It'd barely ended when my friends began ringing, hoping to get the scoop."

"Should see some clients come of it," Edmond told me. "Have any reached out to ya?"

"Around a dozen, including Kiernan Moffat." I told them about the *client* who'd just left. I heaved an overwhelmed sigh. "I have no clue where to begin researching."

"All we know is the fella was killed after 1928." Biddy snapped her mouth shut. "Janey. I shouldn't be sharing that. It's not public knowledge."

Edmond smiled. "No worries, luv. We won't say a word. Won't even be asking how that date was determined." He gave her a reassuring wink.

"It must be related to a cold case," Rosie said. "I would start by searching for missing persons. I doubt there was a central database or records office for missing persons at that time. They'd have been noted in the local papers."

I nodded. "Ireland *Police Gazette* publications are online for the mid to late eighteen hundreds. The paper was only distributed between police divisions. It included things like reported crimes, wanted criminals, and missing persons. The number of details in an entry makes you hope your ancestors were habitual criminals. Not even the National Library has them on file as recent as 1928. Have to stick with the Westmeath papers."

"Edmond and I could search papers beginning in 1928," Rosie said. "How exciting to help solve a cold-case murder."

"We don't know if it was a murder," I said.

"How couldn't it be?" Rosie asked. "Who'd have been burying a person in their yard otherwise? Certainly wasn't a legal thing to be doing, not even back in those days."

Biddy nodded. "Right? It has to be foul play."

"That'd be a huge help if you two could search newspapers from 1928 on. Be sure to check everywhere, even in the ad section. People sometimes placed ads looking for family members who'd moved away and lost touch."

Reviewing old newspapers was an interesting yet time-consuming task. Even if you knew the death date and an obituary or death notice had been put in the paper, you could spend hours searching for it. The tiny print was often faint or blurred. The notices were squeezed in wherever they would fit—after a front-page article on the Irish Civil War, between ads, and under columns contributed by villages and townlands that noted area deaths. As a genealogist, I sometimes hoped that the person was murdered or died a tragic death so it'd made the paper if an obit hadn't.

Did that make me a pessimist or an optimist?

I turned to Rosie. "If you have a computer, I could give you my account information for Ireland's historical newspaper site."

Edmond didn't own a computer. He'd freaked out when I'd temporarily given him Grandma's computer loaded with her genealogy client files and historical documents when I'd thought I was selling her house and putting items into storage.

"What fun would that be?" Edmond said. "I'd much

prefer the faint musty scent of the library's history room filled with old books and documents than sitting at my kitchen table. And we can accomplish twice as much if we each have our own microfilm viewer."

"I agree." Rosie smiled. "Being a detective isn't nearly as exciting as it used to be. Nowadays so much of the research is conducted on a computer rather than snooping around gathering evidence and questioning suspects. Hercule Poirot would turn over in his grave."

If he wasn't a fictional character.

I also preferred scrolling through microfilm in the library's history room. I hadn't always been a great research assistant for Grandma. Staying focused on the task at hand was difficult when I'd come across an interesting tidbit. Like a local column about who was doing what with whom. Even when the people had been dead for years, it was difficult not to get sucked into the drama.

The couple was off to the library to find a missing person notice, dirt on the Dunphy family, or any area news that sounded suspicious and might be a clue.

Biddy read a text, then sprang from the couch. "I hate to ditch ya, but work couldn't find anyone to cover for me, so I offered to be going in. Feeling much better now that I didn't look like a complete muppet through the entire show and can say the teleprompter was banjaxed. Need the money and don't want to be losing my job. And best be calling Collin." A goofy grin spread across her face at the mention of her boyfriend.

"Do you need a ride?"

"Nope, I'm grand. Going to use my mum's car. She's working at the pub today."

"I'll be spending most of the day putting together Ernest Dunphy's family tree and visiting the Kilcarrigy cemetery. Want to go with me to see Kiernan tonight and pick up what historical documents and clues he might have found?"

"That'd be fab. Half four in the convenience store's lot."

While Biddy slipped on my yellow wellies instead of her muddy brown shoes, I grabbed her dress from a lounge chair on the back patio. The wind had died down by the time we'd gotten home, so she'd placed the dress outside hoping the rain would miraculously wash away the mud. Instead, mud puddles had formed on the cream-colored dress. I shook it out, and watermark stains remained. I stuck it in a plastic bag, not wanting Biddy to see it until she was out of my hearing range.

Dressed in my blue fleece jammies, she whisked out the door and headed up the road toward her house.

I checked on my tartan gown hanging on the shower door in the master bathroom. Using a towel, I brushed the dried mud from its skirt. It looked better than I'd expected. A dry cleaner could undoubtedly have it looking like new. I straightened the small bows on the front of the bodice and swept a finger over the ribbon covering a puffy sleeve. Instead of saving the gorgeous gown for my possible wedding, I had to wear it to every appropriate event. Like conducting castle cemetery tours or attending the Scottish Highland Games? As if I attended fancy balls. I'd have to take ballroom dance classes merely to get some use out of the dress.

I was itching to contact my Scottish family along with the castle hotel's owner, Archie, about the *Roadshow* filming. However, if it fell through, they might have already spent the year's marketing budget advertising the castle's feature on an upcoming episode. I'd wait a few days until I was confident I could trust Kiernan Moffat to hold up his end of the deal. Or when I at least felt more optimistic that he wouldn't have his lawyer deem our contract void in the time it took him to rip it to shreds.

Five

BEFORE I STARTED RESEARCHING the estate's history and Ernest Dunphy's family tree, I had to pop by and see Gretta. I hadn't mentioned my concern to Biddy about Gretta not having contacted me for the scoop on Skelly and about the show's mysterious blackout. Even after a recent group hug at Gretta's son's grave, the two women remained a bit antagonistic. Biddy was jealous of my new friendship with our former enemy.

I zipped through the shower, threw on a red wool sweater and jeans, and headed off for Gretta's house less than ten minutes away. Now when I drove down the narrow road leading to Gretta's, my stomach no longer clenched at the memory of the nasty woman demanding Grandma, Biddy, and I replace every daffodil Biddy and I had yanked up along Gretta's road when we were eight. Discovering that the perky yellow flowers had been a memorial to Gretta's dead son had prompted our group hug in the cemetery.

An impressive wrought-iron gate opened to a paved drive, lined with pumpkins, leading back to the Lynches' two-story stone house with a yellow door and window trim. Dozens of small ghosts hung from the oak trees' branches and flitted in the faint breeze. Fake black tarantulas dotted the spiderwebs blanketing the shrubs. Several happy jack-o'-lanterns sat on the front porch to welcome trick-or-treaters, likely for the first time.

Goodbye Gretta the Grinch and hello Gretta the Good Witch.

Gretta's husband, Tommy, greeted me before I could ring the doorbell. A gray-haired man with a bit of a belly, Tommy's usual happy brown eyes were darkened with worry. He ushered me into the front sitting room.

"So glad ya called in," he said in a hushed voice. "She hasn't gotten off the sofa since yesterday afternoon. Even slept on it in her clothes. Haven't a clue what's wrong. Was grand yesterday when the wee ones were coming 'round in costumes. Never have we had so many. In the past Gretta kept the lights off, the curtains shut. After they stopped coming, she was on the sofa eating leftover sweets and hasn't gotten off it. Not even to go to the loo, I don't think." He rubbed his gray stubbly chin.

"Has she heard about the skeleton discovered over in Kilcarrigy?"

He nodded. "Told her about the yoke this morning. Not even the faintest smile. Brought her scanner in, and she turned it off. Hope you can cheer her up. Maybe talk about being on the tellie last night." He smiled. "You lasses were grand. We watched it, but no reaction from Gretta."

"I'll see what I can do."

Tommy led me back to a daffodil-yellow room. A painting of the flowers hung over a white marble fireplace.

The slim woman was sitting on the cream-colored sofa, unwrapping a full-size chocolate bar, a smear of chocolate on the cushion next to her. A gummy bear clung to the front of her festive green knitted sweater with pumpkins. The past few months, her overprocessed color treatment had faded. Her hair was now a shade *lighter* than my blacktop drive. It hung limp against her shoulders, not in its usual bun.

Unsure what to say, I unwrapped a candy bar and sat in the chair next to her. I savored a bite of milk chocolate, then took the plunge. "Your Halloween decorations are wonderful. Tommy mentioned you had a ton of trick-or-treaters yesterday." I smiled with enthusiasm.

The woman burst into tears, chocolate spittle oozing out the corners of her mouth. I snagged a tissue from a box on the credenza. Before I could hand it to Gretta, she wiped her mouth with a yellow throw blanket next to her.

Hopefully, I wasn't too late to help the poor woman.

I grabbed the box of tissues and sat on the couch next to her. "What's wrong?"

She choked back a sob. "All the wee ones"—she inhaled a shaky breath—"were so cute in their costumes yesterday."

"I'm sure they were. Did something happen?"

"I'll never be a granny."

Ahh... Last Christmas, when Edmond and I had questioned Gretta while attempting to identify Finn O'Brien's father, she'd mistakenly assumed we were implying Finn was her daughter's son. After Gretta kicked us out of the house, Edmond and I'd pieced together part of the puzzle, and Biddy's mom had filled in the rest of what she believed had happened. Nearly thirty years ago Gretta's daughter, Maeve, had become pregnant after graduating. Gretta had shipped her off to England to live with relatives and put the baby up for adoption. The child's father was rumored to have been a married man. In a small community where everybody knew everybody else's business, I was shocked that the details of Maeve's pregnancy had remained a secret, especially if the father of the child was a *local* married man.

"Richard is dead, and the other two lads will never have children. Now Maeve is too old for another. I was a horrible person, forcing my daughter to give up her child, my grandchild."

"I'm sure you did the best you could at the time. After all, you were still recovering from Richard's death." Her son had died at nineteen.

She burst into tears again.

I took another bite of chocolate. I'd be better off keeping my mouth shut and polishing off the bowl of candy bars with her. I didn't know the details of the situation with her daughter, but I knew Gretta hadn't been a very nice person until after she'd accidentally run Finn O'Brien off the road last Christmas.

"Losing Richard should have made me realize how important family is no matter what the situation. How couldn't I have realized that? I've lost a daughter and my only chance for a grandchild because of it. She only comes home to see Tommy. She couldn't care less if I'm dead. Wouldn't even come to my wake or funeral, I'm sure." She sobbed uncontrollably.

I hugged Gretta, unsure how to console the poor woman. She'd never have the chance to know her grandchild, unless... "You could take a DNA test and maybe find him or her."

My heart raced, unsure if I should have made the offer.

Gretta's tear-filled gray eyes glistened with hope. "Think we might find the child, do you? It's a boy."

I shrugged. "If he's taken a DNA test, he'll be a close enough match to easily determine your relationship."

That didn't mean the child was Maeve's. One of Gretta's sons could have an unknown child out there. Not that Gretta wouldn't welcome any grandchild with open arms at this point in her life.

"I haven't a clue about DNA testing." Gretta plucked the gummy bear from her sweater. "Could you be helping me?"

"Of course. Just remember, it'll be hit or miss if your grandchild has taken a test, especially depending on where in the world he lives. Ancestry DNA testing isn't as popular in England or Ireland as it is in the US."

Gretta threw the yellow blanket off her lap and scurried from the room. Moments later she returned with her credit card and laptop. She logged in to the computer and handed it over to me.

"Are you sure about this?" I asked.

I wasn't.

She gave her head a definitive nod. "Absolutely."

"You need to be prepared for every possible outcome." I reminded her about a test revealing my dad wasn't my biological father and turning my world upside down. "My situation has turned out fine so far with Ian, but it might not have for many reasons. Your daughter's child might resent you and Maeve. And Maeve might be upset you took a test without her blessing."

"Not like I could damage our relationship any further. Perhaps taking a test will help mend it."

"Do you know who the child's father is?"

Gretta shook her head.

"I'm guessing you know he was rumored to have been a married man?"

She nodded.

"If he turns out to be a local married man, that could cause a lot of upset. You might not only be changing three families' lives but an entire community."

"I'll cross that road when I get there. If I believe the results will cause more harm than good, then we'll be keeping it to ourselves. You can't be telling Tommy or Biddy about this."

"I promise."

I created Gretta's account on Ancestry.com. Once the results were received, I could download her DNA to several sites for free. She handed over her credit card, and I ordered a test with expedited shipping.

"How long will this take?" she asked anxiously.

"The test will be here within a week. The results average six to eight weeks."

"Six to eight weeks means I'll be receiving them around Christmas." She smiled, giving my arm an appreciative squeeze. "It'll be a blessing. I know it will."

Last Christmas I'd buried Grandma and Gretta had been charged with an accidental hit-and-run. Her DNA results couldn't make this holiday season any worse than the last one.

Could they?

I sipped my hot tea while peering out the kitchen window at Pinky on the front lawn, scarfing up the Froot Loops I'd just tossed out to him. Watching the sheep enjoy his treat eased the chest pain I'd been experiencing since leaving Gretta's. I assured myself that Gretta's DNA results would lead to her locating her grandchild and repairing her relationship with her daughter. That they'd be one big happy family.

Identifying people via DNA testing couldn't change what happened in the past. However, it would certainly impact some people's actions now and in the future. Criminals might think twice before committing a crime. A spouse before having an affair only for a child, like me, to learn about it twenty-five years later thanks to a DNA test. Hiding secrets wasn't nearly as easy as it was even twenty years ago or whenever Skelly was buried.

Sitting at the table, I booted my laptop, envious of Pinky outside sunning himself. The sooner I pieced together Ernest Dunphy's family tree, the sooner I could explore Kilcarrigy's cemetery and perhaps discover a family plot. I also needed access to Kilcarrigy's church baptism, marriage, and death records, which were only online until 1890.

Although the library's history room had many of the county's cemetery transcriptions on file, I preferred the thrill of traipsing through a cemetery. Between the gravestones and church records, I might complete much of the family's tree. Witnesses and sponsors were family members or close friends. The people wouldn't be alive, but a child might be who'd heard family gossip. Not necessarily that Uncle Ernest had buried Cousin Martin under the garden shed. But a clue the person might not even be aware was a clue. People were much more willing to talk decades later to a friendly face like mine rather than an intimidating garda.

Ireland's 1901 and 1911 censuses would likely provide the most information in one spot. The 1921 census had been delayed until 1926 because of Ireland's War of Independence and the Civil War that followed it. The government's one-hundred-year privacy law prevented the 1926 census from being available to the public until 2026. Just my luck, seeing as the 1926 one could contain clues for a man two years later with a 1928 penny.

Thankfully, Dunphy was an uncommon last name. In the 1911 census, the only Ernest Dunphy noted was a four-year-old living in Kilcarrigy with his parents and an older sister. More siblings had likely been born after him. Too bad I couldn't get a peek at the 1926 census. Two boarders and a visitor were also listed. Non-family members could have lived on the estate in later years when Skelly was killed.

Had the family been living on the estate in 1911?

According to one census form, the family resided in a ten- to twelve-room first-class house with eight front windows; walls constructed of stone, brick, or concrete; and a roof made of slate, iron, or tiles. That sounded like Kiernan Moffat's estate. Prior to a series of land acts, most Irish were tenant farmers renting from English landlords until circa 1900. Maybe that was how the family had acquired the estate. Killed a nasty landlord whom they'd rented from for years and buried him under the shed.

I wasn't ruling anything out at this point.

Except the landlord should have been long gone by 1928.

Ireland's civil records began in 1864. An online index listed records a hundred years after a person's birth, seventy-five years after marriage, and fifty years after a death. Some areas offered an online image of the record, whereas others had to be ordered. Only fifteen Dunphy deaths were recorded in the county from 1911 to 1970, including Ernest's father and mother. That ruled out the father being Skelly. Ernest had been the informant on both records. Had he been the only family member in the area or the only one alive at the time? Any sisters had likely married and changed their surname. Kiernan had mentioned he was about eleven or twelve when Ernest died. The appraiser's online celebrity bio confirmed he was born in 1974, meaning Ernest died circa 1985.

Ernest's father died in 1946 before Ernest married Kiernan's grandma in the late 1940s. His mother had likely lived with the couple. The parents' obits might list all the children's names. I'd have Edmond and Rosie add that to their task list. Next, I needed to create a private Dunphy tree on Ancestry.com with the newly discovered information.

My phone rang. Biddy.

"Solved the mystery, have ya?" she asked.

"Visited Gretta so got a late start." I snapped my mouth shut.

"Why were you at *her* house?"

"Was worried I hadn't heard from her about the skeleton or the show cutting out last night."

"I'm sure she's grand."

"No, she isn't."

"Why, what's wrong?" Biddy's snarky tone vanished.

"Just personal stuff."

"What personal stuff?" Biddy demanded.

"Stuff I promised not to tell."

"If she swore you to secrecy, she certainly didn't expect you not to tell me. We tell each other everything."

"Actually, she specifically mentioned not to tell you."

"Serious, are ya? As if she said, 'Now don't you be telling Biddy this'?"

Pretty much.

"It's no big deal," I said. "She doesn't want me mentioning it to Tommy either."

"Expecting you to keep a secret from her husband is one thing, but from your best friend quite another. Still your best friend, aren't I?"

I rolled my eyes.

"And here I thought the woman and I were getting on grand after our group hug and she confiding in us about the daffodils and her son Peter."

Her son was Richard.

"Can't believe you and Gretta are sharing secrets behind my back."

"It's not behind your back when it has nothing to do with you. It's about Gretta. Drop it. I'm going to go to the Kilcarrigy cemetery and check the parish records. Are you still meeting up with me after work to visit Kiernan?"

"Why? Gretta not able to join you?" Biddy harrumphed. "I'll meet you at the store half four."

Click.

I felt like I was back in junior high.

I'd hated junior high!

Finn O'Brien, whom I'd dated for a bit, and I had broken up because of my friendship with Gretta. He'd disapproved of our relationship after the woman had nearly killed him. Honestly, that was merely the tip of the iceberg that sank our relationship before it even became one. We'd both just been flirting with the idea of one. Biddy and I wouldn't end a friendship over this, but we might end up in a brawl!

Before leaving I watched a few DIY videos on how to remove wooden floorboards without power tools. Not only had I never used an electric tool, I had to be discreet pulling up one of Kiernan's floorboards to take a peek underneath.

Fifteen minutes later, I'd searched Grandpa's old tools in the shed and found a putty knife, hammer, and crowbar. The putty knife was as close as I could come to the recommended sturdier scraper. I'd ask Kiernan permission before removing a floorboard. If he said no, I wasn't sure what I'd do. If there was something under the floor, it had to be valuable or confidential, otherwise why hide it?

Because there hadn't been room under the garden shed?

What if Biddy and I tore up a floorboard and discovered another skeleton?

What was the chance of uncovering two skeletons buried on one estate? Yet who'd have thought I'd find *one* skeleton?

Six

KILCARRIGY'S white church and adjoining cemetery were on the edge of town. Nobody answered the door at the rectory, a large white house, so I checked inside the church. Rural churches often remained open so parishioners could light a candle and say a prayer or confess to the priest. Inside, a chill raced through me, and I snuggled into my red wool sweater. The faint sunlight filtering through the stained-glass windows did little to warm the place. Plaques under two windows and a statue noted the Dunphy family had donated the items.

Had the family been trying to redeem themselves? I couldn't imagine they weren't somehow involved in Skelly's death, which occurred after 1928. What was the chance that the victim had a sixty-year-old coin in his pocket if he'd died after Kiernan's grandma, Isobel Moffat Dunphy, in 1992? Following her death, the house had remained unoccupied. If the bones were only thirty years old, wouldn't the anthropologist have determined they were well under seventy years and launched an investigation?

I walked through the cemetery's open gate, my heart racing. Entering a graveyard for the first time was an adrenaline rush. A bigger rush than my first kiss or first date. That said a lot about my love life and why I shouldn't hold off wearing my tartan gown until my wedding. It might hang in my closet until I was buried in it.

A layer of pebbles or colored-glass chippings covered the ground in front of many of the newer graves toward the front. An Irish tradition. I headed straight toward the back. I often felt Grandma was guiding me through a cemetery. Like when I'd discovered a man's body on my grandparents' graves. Why had I chosen to visit there within an hour after he'd died while digging up the grave to bury the remains of his wife, Grandpa's sister?

Ten minutes and I'd found the Dunphy family plot with three headstones. Ernest and Isobel, his parents, and an unmarried younger sister. That made three children, including the older one from the census, and who knew how many more. I'd have to check civil birth records.

The gravestones were recent, in genealogy terms. I wouldn't have to resort to molding aluminum foil over weathered stones to read the transcriptions. I kept a roll in my car just in case. I snapped shots of the stones and surrounding ones with different surnames that could have been married Dunphy women or other relations.

"Related to 'em, are ya?" an elderly woman's voice startled me from behind.

I turned and smiled at the petite silver-haired woman wrapped in a green knit shawl and holding a bouquet of colorful flowers. "No, I'm not."

"Ah, right, then. Merely curious about the skeleton found on the family's estate?"

"I'm a friend of a family member."

"Kind of you to be paying respects to the family at such a dreadful time." She smiled at Ernest and Isobel's stone. "Was a lovely fella, Ernest Dunphy. Every time he saw me sister and me, he'd give us each a pence for sweets. Of course, a pence bought much more back then than nowadays."

"Did you know the family well?" I asked.

She shook her head. "Merely Ernest. Never saw much of his mum. The rest were gone before my time in the early fifties. Had either died or moved away."

"Do you know of any Dunphys in the area?"

"A Paul Dunphy, but the lad was a blow-in from Wicklow not more than twenty years back. Not a relation that I know of. If yer interested in the family's background, ya should be calling in on Bernie McBride. 'Tis the area's local historian. Used to be the caretaker of the graveyard here."

I liked this Bernie guy already. He was undoubtedly a wealth of information, like Edmond, Ballycaffey's historian.

"Lives in the nursing home at the edge of town. He'd be over the moon to have a lovely young lass like yerself call in on him. Several other locals living there might be older than meself and recall more from that time." She glanced down at her flowers. "Best be putting these on Paddy's grave." She handed me a pink rose from the bouquet. "For all those sweets the fella gave me." She smiled and headed off.

I placed the rose on the grass in front of Ernest and Isobel's stone. I had to meet Biddy in an hour. Best to hold off visiting the home until tomorrow. I didn't want to rush my visit with the historian and other locals who might have clues. They'd also soon be having dinner. I knocked on the rectory door once again but no answer.

I'd have to pop by another day.

Taking advantage of the fresh air and sunshine, I called Dad to tell him about having discovered Skelly. And that my involvement in the investigation was hush-hush. I left out my agreement with Kiernan Moffat and that successfully identifying Skelly could result in the show filming at the castle. Just in case it didn't.

"At least it wasn't an actual body you found this time." Dad's tone was concerned yet calm, considering the subject. "Can't imagine many fathers say that to a daughter."

Two might say it in my case.

However, Ian would likely find my situation disturbing.

"Hope not. I like to think I'm unique. And I wasn't actually the one who found Malcolm, so that's one less."

"Not sure if a skeleton is any less traumatic or not. And suppose it was good timing that the discovery was made *after* the show, not *before* it. You girls looked beautiful. Had expected to see more of Biddy though."

So had I.

"She had a few challenges with the filming."

"Bit of stage fright?"

"Yep, but don't tell her I told you."

"Mum's the word. It's a shame your mom and grandmother weren't still with us. They'd be so proud of you having traced your grandfather's Fitzsimmons line. And not only did you appear on the show but a cowriter as well. I'm proud of you, Mags."

My eyes watered, and a lump of emotion stuck in my

throat. Grandma would have watched the show at McCarthy's or Edmond's while enjoying her Irish coffee. Despite my rocky relationship with Mom, I wanted to believe she'd have stopped comparing me to my college-educated sisters and have encouraged me to continue following my dreams. I wiped a tear from my cheek.

"I'm sure the hotel is seeing plenty of bookings thanks to you," Dad said. "Will have to ask Ian about it when we talk tomorrow."

"You're talking to Ian tomorrow?"

"And Tavish. Planning our golf trip in the spring." He paused. "You're still okay with us taking the trip together?"

"Yeah, of course. Ian and I are fine."

It appeared Dad and Ian were better than *fine*.

At first Dad and I were devastated that Ian and Mom had betrayed Dad, likely in our own home. Later, when the shock and anger had worn off, Dad and Ian forged a friendship, whereas I took the rational approach. On the upside, Ian being my biological father gave Dad and me a blood connection besides our father-daughter emotional bond. It also provided me with insight into my paternal ancestry. However, it was Ava who'd told me that their father was a mix of Scottish and English. And Ian's mother—Ava's stepmother—was English and French. No wonder I was only 8 percent Scottish.

Was I being *too* rational about my relationship with Ian and not emotional *enough*?

"Have you spoken to him lately?" he asked.

"He texted after seeing the show." Texting left less room for awkward silence, saying the wrong thing, or becoming emotional and lashing out. "A golf trip will be great for you guys. You need to take advantage of your retirement."

"*Part-time* retirement."

Dad had announced his part-time retirement after the Murray reunion last month. His first project was helping with the castle refurbishments.

"Figure we'll work the trip around the castle's filming. Do you know when the show might make a final decision on that?"

"Soon."

As soon as I identified Skelly and Kiernan held up his end of the deal. I hoped Dad hadn't invested his entire retirement account on this venture. He was much too conservative for that.

Wasn't he?

Dressed in blue Scooby-Doo scrubs, Biddy was perusing the ice-cream cooler inside the Kilcarrigy convenience store. She greeted me with a smile, appearing to be over her childish "you like Gretta better than me" rant. I gave her a status report on my Dunphy family research and encounter with the woman at the cemetery.

"Ah, wish I could be going with you to the home tomorrow to chat with folks, but I have to work."

"How'd it go today?"

"Grand. Telling everyone the teleprompter was banjaxed worked. They all felt bad for me, except that wretched Hannah Riley. Merely jealous that I'd been on the show a second time, even if it was a small role. Wait until she hears I'm going to be on a third time."

"Don't be telling anyone about that until it's confirmed."

Even if the castle filming was a go, I'd have to do an awful lot of sucking up for Kiernan to approve Biddy appearing on another episode. Like proving Skelly was Sir Arthur Conan Doyle, author of *Sherlock Holmes*. That the man had secretly been Kiernan's blood relative and wanted his burial to be his last mystery for someone to one day solve.

Biddy opted for an ice-cream sandwich, while I grabbed a to-go cup of tea and a bag of Taytos.

"I should get Kiernan a bite to eat. He's likely been hiding out at the estate all day with little or no food in the fridge for his unplanned stay there." His permanent residence was hours away down in Cork.

"As if the fella would fancy takeaway cuisine. Doubt he'd even like the lasagna, which is absolutely lovely."

I nodded. My dinner often consisted of an entrée from the chain store's takeaway section, like their signature lasagna or a custom-made salad. I bought the appraiser a bag of chocolate buttons and mixed nuts.

Biddy sat in the passenger seat, licking the vanilla ice cream from the chocolate wafers. "Sorry I was a bit cheeky about Gretta on the phone. Have to admit, been worried about her since. She's not deathly ill or anything, is she?"

I smiled at Biddy's genuine concern. "No, she's not."

At least I hoped that wasn't Gretta's reason for wanting to find her grandchild. Would be sad if it was the woman's last dying wish after she'd turned over a new leaf less than a year ago.

"You'd tell me if it was something dreadful, right?"

I nodded, despite being unsure whether I'd break my promise to Gretta or not.

Biddy smiled and slipped her cell phone from the front pocket of her purse. "I haven't had time to do damage control but been checking social media. People are brutal. The newspapers aren't much better. 'One Skeleton in a Yard May Uncover Dozens in the Closet of Celebrity Kiernan Moffat.' I hope he's staying off the internet."

Dusk settling in, we arrived at the estate to find the driveway entrance partially flooded and four orange construction cones off to the side.

"Bet he forgot to block it, being frazzled this morning." Biddy hopped out and lined the cones across the drive behind us.

Tree branches and debris scattered across the muddy gravel made for a bit of a bumpy ride. Last night the film crew had dragged several larger limbs aside to make their getaway down the narrow lane lined with woods. The end of the drive opened up into the parking area. The large Georgian-style stone house wasn't nearly as eerie without gale-force winds howling through the creepy trees or a skeleton buried under one of them. However, it was creepy that a young couple was taking selfies in front of the crime scene tape.

Biddy glanced from the couple's blue car to Kiernan's Mercedes and the gray wreck he was driving that morning. "Where's my car?"

I shrugged, stepping from the vehicle.

"The garda never mentioned taking it somewhere else. What if some other nosey eejits snooping around the crime scene decided they wanted a souvenir and nicked it?"

The appraiser dashed out the front door wearing a green velvet monogrammed robe and matching slippers. It was a step up from his sloppy sweatsuit earlier. Still, several steps down from the pretentious man's typical designer attire.

He flung his arms wildly in the air at the couple taking selfies. "What the hell do you think you're doing?"

The woman raised her phone to snap a picture or to videotape the crazy man charging at them, cussing up a storm. Either would go viral on social media in a matter of minutes.

Biddy snatched the phone from the woman's hand. "You need to be having some respect for both the living and the dead. We wouldn't have dreamed of taking a snap of the yoke when we found it."

"You discovered the skeleton?" the woman asked in awe, which was better than tackling Biddy for her phone.

I shot Biddy a cautioning glance.

She shook her head. "I said even *if* we'd found the yoke, we wouldn't have taken a snap."

The couple shared skeptical glances.

While the woman and Biddy fought over the phone, I cut Kiernan off at the pass. The overpowering stench of whiskey filled my nose. "Get back inside before that couple gets you on video sounding like a raving lunatic, saying something you'll regret." I eyed his mud-covered velvet slippers and the bottom of his robe. "Your outfit alone would go viral."

The man tightened the sash on his robe and squared his shoulders, attempting an air of respectability.

"Biddy and I'll get rid of them," I said.

He spun around and bolted toward the house, nearly slipping in the mud, twice.

I joined Biddy and the couple, arguing.

"If I give you back your mobile, ya aren't leaving until the snaps are deleted," Biddy said.

The woman gave Biddy the stink eye. "It's my mobile. Can do with it as I please." The woman was a scrappy little thing, but Biddy was scrappier.

"If you don't delete them, I'll contact the guards and tell them we found you trespassing at the scene of an investigation."

I snapped a picture of the couple and their car's license plate.

Biddy smirked. "Now we have the evidence to prove it."

"Just give me the bloody yoke," the guy said. "A few snaps aren't worth all this drama."

Biddy handed him the phone, and we watched until he deleted every estate pic. They marched over to their car. The woman slid in behind the steering wheel and slammed the driver's door shut.

"Eejits." Biddy smiled proudly. "My first act as social media damage control manager."

"Awesome job," I said.

We did a high five.

However, the couple was still here. Their car's rear tires were spinning in the mud. Biddy and I glared at the tires as if to harness our psychic powers and send the car zipping down the drive.

The guy climbed out of the vehicle, annoyed. "Mind giving us a bit of help, would you?"

"Mad, are ya?" Biddy said. "As if we should be pushing your car when you're trespassing on private property."

He gestured to a black brace covering his forearm and lower hand. "Sprained my wrist. I can't be driving or pushing."

Biddy and I glared at him.

"Right, then." He relaxed his other arm over the open car door. "Guess we'll just be hanging here until the mud dries up."

Biddy and I stalked over to the car, swearing like the lads at closing time. Panic seized the guy's face. He hopped into the car and slammed the door. Raging with adrenaline, Biddy and I could have pushed a semitruck from a sinkhole. The car lurched from the ruts, spitting mud all over us. As they drove off, the jerk leaned out the window and snapped our picture.

"Bloody eejit!" Biddy screamed at the car disappearing down the drive. "If that shows up under hashtag MoffatMayhem, I'll hunt the fella down!"

We stood paralyzed at the thought of our photo going viral on social media.

"I'm sure the snap is a total blur, with the fella leaning out the window. And he was likely taking a shot of the crime scene tape, not us."

I nodded, glancing over my shoulder at the taped-off area behind us. I brushed splattered mud from my face. "Besides, nobody would recognize us covered in mud."

Using a packet of wipes from my car, Biddy and I cleaned off our faces and hands. Biddy flicked big globs of mud from her Scooby-Doo scrubs while I plucked a twig from my wool sweater. We marched inside and removed our shoes despite the muddy slipper prints trailing across the Turkish rug and up the wooden stairs. Kiernan was in the library, pouring a whiskey from a crystal decanter and listening to classical music. He eyed our soiled clothing and took a gulp of liquor.

I handed him the bag of mixed nuts and chocolate buttons. "You need to eat something and drink some strong tea."

"And be staying off social media if this is what it's doing to ya." Biddy gestured to his outfit. "I can't be quitting my nursing job to be handling your media circus full time."

He took another gulp of whiskey. "A garda just stopped to inform me that the fella in the yard had a cracked skull. Had likely been struck with a heavy object." He popped a chocolate button in his mouth.

"Like a garden shovel?" Biddy said.

"Quite the inconsiderate killer, not having provided more clues, such as the murder weapon," Kiernan quipped. "Merely a pence piece. They're waiting to release any information to the public."

"I'm sure most people already figured the person hadn't died from natural causes, being buried under the shed," I said.

We certainly had.

"Call me an optimist," Kiernan said. "I was holding out hope for a happier ending."

"Maybe it was an accidental death," Biddy said. "Maybe he fell in the shed and hit his head on a shovel. A Dunphy was afraid it'd look like murder, so they buried him."

"Is that all the garda told you?" I asked.

"That was quite enough for now, seeing as I'm down to one bottle of whiskey."

I snatched the decanter off the cart before he could pour

another glass. "This is a crappy situation, but you need to get a grip. What if that couple had taken a video and it went viral? Don't allow this to destroy your career or your life. You'd be best off getting back to work and giving people less to talk about rather than hiding out here and allowing them to concoct all kinds of wild tales."

"Go to work and be verbally attacked by the media and my coworkers? Think I'd prefer to lie low for a few days until the hype dies down."

"You're going to let that dope who doesn't know the author of *Dr. Zhivago* fill in for you?" Biddy said.

The man let out a defeated sigh. "Haven't a choice. The producer has requested that I keep my distance from the filming location for the time."

Biddy and I exchanged worried glances. What if the show mandated he take a temporary leave of absence or, even worse, let him go? That would be bad for all of us.

"This is a pretty obvious spot to be hiding out," Biddy said. "Not too clandestine. At least hire security to guard the place. And why isn't there a garda down by the crime scene if it's still taped off?"

"Excellent question. Let's drink to that." Kiernan polished off his whiskey.

"And where's my car?"

He shrugged. "It was gone when I left this morning. I'm assuming the forensics team collected it."

Biddy's gaze narrowed. "And took it where?"

"Wherever they take evidence."

"It's not evidence."

"You'll have to ask the garda."

Biddy gave him the evil eye.

Kiernan ignored her frustration and turned to me. "I'm assuming you haven't determined the deceased's identity or you'd have brought champagne rather than chocolate buttons and nuts."

I updated him on my Dunphy family tree and having confirmed that the family lived on the estate at the time of the 1901 and 1911 censuses. "I'm going to visit a local historian at the nursing home tomorrow."

The man's blue eyes widened. "You can't be discussing this with some random locals."

"I doubt they're talking about anything else. I'm sure the discovery is the most excitement the residents have had in years. They might provide some insight. I'll be discreet. Not like I'm going to interrogate people and tell them I'm investigating the skeleton."

I didn't dare admit I'd discussed the Dunphy family with the woman at the cemetery who'd recommended I visit the local historian. Also, that Edmond and Rosie were researching newspapers for missing persons or other clues. However, it didn't appear Kiernan had taken time to have his lawyer draft up a contract, including a confidentiality clause. The old Kiernan Moffat wouldn't have allowed me in the house without having signed the legal document. I wasn't sure about the current man, in many respects.

"Biddy is researching papers starting in 1928 for missing persons or other clues," I lied.

He gazed expectantly at Biddy. "Well, what have you found?"

"Ah, nothing yet, but I'll be working on it more tonight."

I crossed my fingers that Edmond and Rosie turned up

something soon. I'd have heard from them if they already had.

"I put together what family records and history I could find." Kiernan gestured to a small stack of papers, books, and a photo album on the desk. "Have a few more items in the other room. Also need to ring work." He left.

I slipped the putty knife, hammer, and crowbar from my tote.

"Fair play to ya," Biddy said.

"I'd planned on asking for permission, but I don't want to send him over the edge."

Biddy nodded. "It's for his own good. If there's nothing under the floor, we can slip the board back in place and he'll never know."

I took a step, then paused. "What if it's another skeleton?"

"Janey," Biddy muttered. "Hadn't thought of that. Our agreement was based on identifying Skelly—that's it. If it's a second skeleton, we'll replace the board and tell him about it after the show films at Dalwade Castle."

Biddy and I bolted across the room. We dropped to our knees and rapped on the floorboards until hearing a hollow sound beneath one. My heart raced. I wedged the putty knife between two boards with the widest gap and pounded the wooden handle as quietly as possible. The gap widened. I slipped the crowbar between the boards and carefully wrenched it. Biddy snatched the lamp off the end table and directed the light under the floor.

We gasped at the sight of a cast-iron safe, then sighed with relief that we hadn't uncovered another body.

"I bet it contains money or family jewels," Biddy said. "It must be worth a ton of quid, or why hide it under the floor?"

"I'd prefer a written confession by the killer who buried Skelly under the shed."

"What are you doing?" Kiernan glared at the crowbar in my hand and the removed board on the floor.

"There's a safe under here," Biddy said. "Now aren't you happy we followed our instincts like good detectives should?"

He marched over and studied the safe.

"It could contain clues," I said.

Biddy nodded. "Or valuables."

"Or more bloody bones," he snapped. "Put that board back in place." He marched over to the desk, then slid his curious gaze toward the exposed area beneath the floor. "Besides, it's likely locked."

"We could take off a few more boards and find out," I said. "It'll be easy enough to put them back in place."

He rubbed his unshaven chin, still eyeing the floor. "Be careful not to split a board. Wouldn't be easy to repair or match that wood." He watched as I carefully pried off two more boards. He attempted to open the safe. "Locked."

"You must know a safe cracker," Biddy said.

He scowled. "I most certainly do not."

"Then I'm sure you know someone who does. Or do you have any firecrackers or dynamite around?"

"Even if I did, I'm not about to blow up the safe and whatever is inside, not to mention the floor."

Biddy nodded. "Suppose not."

"Here, I'll find a video on opening safes." I slipped my phone from my purse. After watching several videos, I quickly became disheartened. "We need to call a locksmith."

"A bit late in the evening for that," Kiernan said.

Biddy shook her head. "Locksmiths work all hours of the day and night. People are always getting locked out of their homes or businesses, especially after the pubs close."

"Where are we going to find a discreet locksmith?" he said. "I certainly don't want more publicity."

Rosie's brother Albert would likely have occasional need for one to open old safes he'd purchased. I called the antique dealer. He recommended an elderly locksmith who didn't have email, so he certainly wasn't active on social media. I phoned the man, who promised to arrive within the hour.

While waiting for him, Kiernan polished off two more whiskeys. Biddy attempted to crack the safe's combination using Ernest's and Isobel's birth and death years along with their marriage and any other years I could recall from my research.

I sifted through the stack of historical records on the desk. The album contained several family photos of the parents and four kids without names or dates. I'd accounted for three kids. A 1915 photo of the home's exterior and outbuildings included a shed under the large oak tree. Kiernan confirmed it was the garden shed he'd recently torn down, meaning the building had been there in 1928. I skipped over the family's grocery store's business ledgers, which I hoped I'd never have to open. Accounting was the least favorite part of my genealogy business. I left other random records to sift through later.

As promised, the locksmith arrived almost an hour after I'd called. Not only did the elderly man not have an email address, he didn't have a driver's license. His wife dropped him off while she ran to the convenience store. Having one more person privy to the situation nearly sent Kiernan over the edge.

Within fifteen minutes, the man had the safe open. He enjoyed a whiskey while waiting for his ride, and we peeked inside the safe. Biddy and Kiernan were disappointed it contained a bunch of papers and documents rather than family jewels or money. But my heart raced. I inhaled the intoxicating scent of old, musty papers as if I were a treasure hunter discovering a sunken ship filled with gold.

The locksmith's wife returned and got stuck partway down the drive. Biddy and I pushed the vehicle out of the mud while Kiernan remained by a toasty fire enjoying another whiskey. When I made it home, I would throw wellies, large plastic garbage bags, and a change of clothes into my trunk.

I'd better get more out of all this than building up my upper-body strength.

Seven

AFTER LEAVING KIERNAN'S, we popped by the Kilcarrigy Garda station located in a former cottage. Neither Garda Higgins's car nor Biddy's sat in the empty lot. The place was closed for the evening. Biddy called the garda, the same one who'd given us a ride home after her car was held for further investigation. She heard his voicemail and about lost it. She left him a message politely inquiring on the location of her vehicle. She hung up, fuming, and I had to talk her out of calling 9-9-9. I promised we'd track it down tomorrow.

Since it was nearly nine o'clock, Biddy and I stopped off at the pub for a cider and pizza. Her mom, Ita, was behind the bar. The festive orange-colored streaks in the hairdresser's blond bob coordinated nicely with her green-and-orange floral blouse. She was chatting with Johnny and Beckham. My nicknames for the older men were nicer than the ones they'd given me. Defender of the Dead and Tombstone Terminator.

Johnny always wore John Deere T-shirts and Beckham wore soccer jerseys, but he didn't resemble the famous player in the least. The men resembled each other. Short and stocky with receding gray hairlines.

Ita's curious gaze narrowed on our muddy appearance.

"Don't ask," Biddy said.

"Can't be any worse than spending the day here listening to skeleton theories until your head is about to explode."

"Ya haven't heard the best one." Johnny turned to his buddy. "Remember back thirty years or so that annoying fella who'd come 'round every week trying to sell ya something? Like those fancy teas. Told him no thanks. I was grand drinking me Barry's every morning. The next week he called in wanting to sell me a box of Barry's for fifty pence more than in the grocer's."

His friend nodded. "Remember him well. Once got what I thought was a great deal on tomatoes till Mary be asking why I'd picked her entire lot of tomatoes when they weren't ripe. Hadn't known she'd planted tomatoes that year. Turned out the fella had sold me our own bloody tomatoes. Course I didn't be telling Mary. Wouldn't have heard the end of it."

"Betcha he nicked some crisps from Dunphy's shop, then tried selling 'em back to them not knowing he was at the grocer's house. The Dunphy man stuffed a bag of crisps in the fella's mouth, and he choked on it. Always wondered why he suddenly stopped coming 'round."

"Thought I heard the fella was struck by a lorry down near Cullenroche. Figured it was no accident."

Ita let out an exhausted groan and refilled the men's pints. "Here, it's on the house. Go play darts and give me a rest. Gonna go mad if I have to listen to one more story."

The men thanked Ita and headed over to the game board.

"That idea wasn't nearly as crazy as some I've heard," Ita said. "Like an alien abducted one of the Dunphy lads. Then the spaceship ran out of gas on takeoff, and they killed the alien and buried it. Or the Dunphys were part of the IRA and the remains are those of a British secret agent."

The lucky penny popped into my head. What if the 1928 coin for the new Free Irish State had been symbolic? The killer had buried it with Skelly to never let the man forget Ireland was free of English rule.

Or was that as farfetched as the alien theory?

"Heard from Ian lately?" Ita asked.

I nodded. "A few texts about the show."

"Ah, that's grand. As long as you're keeping in touch, you can take your time and see where the road leads."

"Yeah. Never thought the road would lead to him."

Ita had been my mom's best friend growing up. She was one of the first people I'd questioned about my biological father's identity. I'd thought maybe Mom had hooked up with an old flame on a visit to Ireland. Ita had recalled the guy she'd dated before meeting my dad had moved to Australia to work on a pearl farm and then to New Zealand to harvest kiwis. Last Ita had heard, he was a bird-watching guide in Papua New Guinea. The man's wanderlust and lack of job stability had made him a prime candidate for my father. Precisely how I'd envisioned my father, rather than a stable history professor who'd lived in Edinburgh for twenty years. Ian's adventurous brother, Tavish, seemed more in my genes. However, I loved history...

Here I went rationalizing my relationship with Ian again.

Gretta entered the pub dressed in tan slacks and a green wool sweater, her dark hair up in a loose bun.

Johnny and Beckham's conversation ceased, and they stared at the woman. As far as I knew, this was only Gretta's second time in McCarthy's. The first time was this past summer when she was helping me solve my Fitzsimmons family mystery.

Gretta slid onto a barstool and joined us.

Biddy smiled at her. "Fancy a cup of tea?"

Gretta blinked in surprise. "That'd be lovely."

"On the house." Biddy went behind the bar, added fresh water to the electric kettle, and flipped the switch. "Prefer Barry's, or I have some flavored teas in back from a specialty shop in Dublin. Peppermint, lemon, a few others."

Not only was Biddy making Gretta complimentary tea but also offering her one from her personal stash?

Gretta smiled. "Barry's would be lovely."

Biddy turned away, and Gretta gave me a curious look.

I shrugged.

"I was passing by and saw your car. Thought I'd stop. Never asked about the skeleton found over in Kilcarrigy. Guessing you're in the know, seeing as you were there last evening."

Gretta sat on the edge of her stool while I filled her in on our involvement with the discovery and attempt to identify Skelly. I swore her to secrecy.

"How exciting. Would love to be helping."

Gretta was likely trying to stay occupied while anxiously awaiting her DNA test. She'd completed her thousand hours of community service work for her involvement with Finn's accident in record time. I didn't want to throw the woman back into a funk by keeping her off the case. Yet Kiernan would flip out if he knew Edmond and Rosie were also privy to my investigation.

However, the more help I had, the quicker I could identify Skelly. Edmond and Rosie were dividing and conquering the newspapers as quickly as they could. It averaged an hour to carefully review two to three papers. That only added up to fifteen or twenty papers per person during library hours. And there were two weekly county papers at that time.

"You could help research newspapers," I told Gretta.

"That'd be grand," Biddy said. "I'm quite busy managing the social media damage control department." She smiled proudly.

"Edmond and Rosie are helping as well. You could start with papers in 1940 and search forward. I could give you my account information for the online historical newspapers site and what to be looking for."

Gretta smiled wide. "That'd be grand."

Biddy set the cup of tea in front of Gretta, including two ginger biscuits on the saucer. She added milk and sugar to the woman's liking.

"Anything else I can be getting ya?" Biddy asked.

Gretta's curious gaze narrowed on Biddy, then me. "You promised not to be telling her."

I crossed my finger over my chest. "I didn't tell her a thing."

"Mags didn't say a word, except that you're a bit down. Can't I merely be worried about ya?"

Gretta took a sip of tea while eyeing Biddy with suspicion.

"Fine." Biddy snatched a cookie from the saucer and took a bite.

I was busy enough without adding referee to my job roles. Like reviewing the documents from Kiernan Moffat and his safe, sifting through my potential-client emails, planning the cemetery project... I gave Gretta the info for my historical Irish newspapers account, bought three bags of Taytos, and left the two women to duke it out.

At home I changed into flannel jammies, sat on the couch with my computer on my lap, and sifted through several dozen emails from potential clients. A third of them requested help with obtaining records and info they could easily find online, mostly civil records. I sent them the links to access the records for free or a nominal fee. I transferred those emails to a Completed folder. Should they need future help with research not found online, they would remember how ethical I was giving them guidance rather than charging them for something they could get for free.

There were numerous requests for wills. People were curious to see if an heirloom, such as mourning jewelry, had unknowingly been left to the family in the past. I sent them the link to the online index. If the requested will was on file, I offered to obtain a copy from the National Archives in Dublin.

A genealogist in Cornwall, England, had watched the show and heard me mention my cousin Simon in Cornwall. He wondered if I wanted to do lunch the next time I was over to visit my cousin. The *first* time I visited that area would be to meet my cousin, not some desperate man who thought we'd have a lot in common. Like taking long walks through cemeteries. Staying up until the wee hours of the morning conducting genealogy research, then sleeping in until noon... I couldn't decide if he was my perfect match or a stalker. I double-checked that my website didn't disclose any clues as to where I lived. Yet rather than deleting the guy's email, I moved it to a Pending folder.

A spam email offered 50 percent off on marketing my genealogy business. As if I needed to advertise for more clients. Delete!

I filed the emails. The Pending folder contained a dozen potential clients I'd review further later. At least I would sleep better not feeling so overwhelmed. Except I had to get up in five hours to work on the cemetery project before heading to the Kilcarrigy nursing home.

My computer dinged the arrival of an email. Thankfully, in my personal account not my business one.

The email was from Ian.

My heart raced. I'd only received a half dozen texts or emails from him since learning of our relationship over a month ago. Two of them in the past two days. He thanked me again for introducing Dalwade Castle to millions of television viewers. Since the Halloween episode had aired, the hotel had seen a major uptick in bookings. The family was feeling much more optimistic about their investment than they had. And they were hoping to replace the boiler soon.

Interesting that Ian had contacted me about the increased business and refurbs. He was more of a silent investor, uninvolved with the hotel's day-to-day operations. Was he attempting to be more involved in *my* day-to-day operations?

I noticed a PS at the end of the email message.

Just heard about the skeleton found at the filming site. Were you there when it was discovered?

Would Ian find my knack for stumbling across dead people intriguing and amusing, like Dad, or creepy and worrisome? He knew about the dead man on my grandparents' graves. And that Biddy and I had arrived on the scene moments after Ian's brother Malcom was found with a fatal arrow in his chest. Ian was thankful Biddy and I'd solved that mystery. However, he might consider my involvement with a *third* dead body in a matter of months a bit...disturbing and excessive.

Dad was the only one I'd told about Skelly. It was a sensitive situation, and I wasn't going around blabbing about it. Justification at its finest.

Eight

THE FOLLOWING MORNING, my goal was to create the cemetery project Facebook page before heading to the nursing home to visit the historian. I wanted Ava and Rhona to provide input before it went live. Building interest now was critical if the project was going to kick off in late spring. Adding photos of the moss-and-ivy-covered tombstones reminded me of giving Dad, Ian, and Tavish a cemetery tour the night before Ian had falsely confessed to his brother Malcolm's murder. The night before I'd confirmed he was my biological father.

I hadn't replied to Ian's email last night. Discussing Skelly would provide insight into my somewhat peculiar life and shift our hotel business relationship to a more personal one. Once I let him into my personal life, he might want out. If he stuck around, I'd have to determine just how *far* to let him in. What if he started texting or emailing me daily? Or calling instead, worried about what morbid thing had happened to me lately? Dad respected my privacy. What if Ian didn't? What if...

My breathing quickened. I closed my eyes and took several calming breaths.

I wasn't ready to have answers for my *what-ifs*.

I had to *get* ready.

It was too bizarre having Dad golf with Ian when I couldn't even email the man.

After a bit of yoga breathing, I responded to Ian's email, keeping it short and sweet. I shared Biddy's and my involvement in discovering Skelly, leaving out our role in trying to identify the deceased. Chest fluttering, I sent the message, then closed my email in case he responded immediately. And so I couldn't check every five minutes, waiting for a response.

Once the actual restoration began, I wasn't sure how often I'd have to visit Scotland. Aer Lingus flights between Dublin and Edinburgh were crazy cheap. An hour round-trip flight averaged forty-five euros, about fifty-two bucks. I stayed for free in the owner Archie's private wing and would have meals included. Luckily, I could conduct much of my Irish genealogy research online while in Scotland. I'd have to select client projects that required limited access to Ireland's archives.

My doorbell rang. It was Biddy on her way to work.

Fuming, she burst into the living room. "That manky scumbag posted the snap of us on Twitter!"

Heart racing, I bolted over to Biddy. My jaw dropped at the photo of us at the estate wearing mud-covered clothes and horrified expressions, the crime scene tape in the background.

Two women dig up body in Kilcarrigy.

"We look surprised from being covered in mud, not because we'd just *uncovered* a buried body!" Biddy's grip tightened on the phone, and I feared she might whip it through a window. "And it wasn't a *body*—it was a *skeleton*. Those bloody hashtags are nasty. Graverobbers, bodysnatchers, skeletonscavengers..."

Way worse than my Tombstone Terminator and Defender of the Dead nicknames!

Biddy paced. "We'll sue that Gaelic Galway Guy for defamation of character. For trespassing on private property. We'll have his Twitter account shut down." Her gaze darted to me. "What if he has other social media accounts? Going to be giving him a piece of my mind while he still has *any* account!" She typed away.

I snatched the phone from her hand. "You can't comment on his post. You're not tagged in it. The jerk doesn't know who we are. Don't tell him. The mud on our faces will make it difficult to identify us. Make sure your Twitter profile doesn't have a picture of you."

"Fine." Biddy grabbed her phone back and scanned through the comments. "Some eejit says we should be put in prison for disturbing the dead. Seriously?" A growl vibrated at the back of Biddy's throat.

"People will realize the story's fake. Skelly was uncovered because of a massive storm and gale-force winds. The weather is calm in this photo."

"Mad, are ya? People are looking at *us*, the body snatchers, not the weather. The snap was posted four hours ago and already has two thousand likes and fifty-three shares. You'd think some celeb had posted it instead of Gaelic Gobshite." Biddy's entire body trembled with anger. "The day couldn't have started any worse. Got an email from the costume shop that the dress costs nearly two hundred euros. Won't be paying that when I'll be tossing the yoke in the rubbish. Have to be getting out those stains." She marched toward the door, glancing over her shoulder. "Have a lovely day!" She slammed the door.

Thanks to Biddy, my day had quickly gone downhill, and I had a migraine coming on from the blood rushing through my head. Taking several calming breaths, I tried to find the upside to our unfortunate situation. On a positive note, we'd diverted the negative publicity from Kiernan Moffat to ourselves. Our photo would undoubtedly go viral within a day.

Were we brilliant at our job or what?

I made some tea and continued adding photos to the cemetery project page.

My phone dinged. A text from Kiernan.

Any clues in my records?

It was only eight o'clock!

I texted back.

Working on it. Off to nursing home soon.

After breakfast, I was eager to hear the theories circulating throughout the nursing home, fingers crossed one of them was right. I grabbed a book for the Kilcarrigy historian. Grandma had given me the book with humorous epitaphs for my tenth birthday. One of my favorites was from a Pennsylvania cemetery.

Here lies the body of Jonathan Blake.
Stepped on the gas instead of the brake.

If I died before Biddy, she'd come up with a great saying for my tombstone. She already had one.

Here lies Mags Murray, who was always great craic.
Until a goat jumped on her back.

A neighbor's goat had once used my back as a springboard. The last thing I saw had better not be a goat charging at me. Biddy would have to come up with another epitaph. Whatever she wrote, it would likely one day end up in a book.

Whispering Manor nursing home was a large older building painted yellow with white trim. An oak tree's red and orange leaves spotted the manicured green lawn, and bushes hugged the front of the home. I pressed a buzzer next to the green-painted door. A friendly woman responded, and I requested a visit with Bernie McBride, explaining I was a fellow historian and genealogist. She buzzed me in and requested I wait in the foyer while she informed the historian about his unscheduled visitor.

Framed landscape photos of Ireland and a list of today's activities hung on the sage-green walls in the small entryway. A pottery class, bingo, and a visiting pianist were on the agenda. I peeked through a doorway into a quiet room where a group of residents were doing tai chi. I smiled, easing out a breath, feeling Zen...

A text dinged on my phone. I ducked away from the doorway, muting the sound. It was Rosie, excited about having possibly found their first clue and hoping for continued success. They planned to stop over after the library closed later that afternoon. What had they discovered?

The nice lady returned with an eightyish-year-old man dressed in tan slacks and a green golf shirt for a popular course in County Cork. Upon seeing me, his blue eyes lit up and he smiled wide.

"Was hoping you'd be calling in for a visit, luv." He spied the book in my hand. "Ah, grand, ya be bringing the book."

I nodded, smiling, a nervous flutter in my chest.

Who did this man think I was?

"Fancy a spot of tea, would ya?" He slipped a warm hand around mine and led me from the foyer.

"That'd be lovely."

Sadly, it didn't appear the man's memory would be up to discussing the Dunphys seventy years ago.

He paraded me down the hall, holding my hand, poking his head into every room to say a quick hello. "Haven't a clue who you are," he told me with a sly wink. "But wasn't about to turn away a lovely lass such as yourself. Oh, the fellas are gonna be jealous. Be the talk of the home for days, I will."

I laughed. "Bet you're quite the ladies' man."

He shrugged. "Don't like to brag."

Outside of a golf putter and balls in a plastic cottage-cheese container, the historian's room reminded me of Edmond's house. Stacks of books and research papers filled every shelf, table, and chair. Same as Edmond, the man had to clear off a chair for me to sit down.

I handed him my book. "Hope you don't already have this one."

He laughed at the book's subject. "Ah, that's brilliant, isn't it now?" He opened the cover to the first page, where Grandma had written me a birthday note. "Right, then. Sure ya want to be trusting me with such an important book, are ya?"

I smiled. "You look like an honest man. And if I can't trust a fellow historian, who can I trust?"

He nodded. "'Tis true."

"My grandma was a genealogist. So am I. I'd be happy to bring more books next time I'm in the area."

He arched a thick white brow. "Exactly what brings you to the area, and more curiously to *me*?"

"I'm researching the Dunphy family."

He grinned. "From the news, are ya?"

"No, just helping a friend of the family. I'm guessing this was the first skeleton found around here."

"Oh, there's often been rumors of bones uncovered, but always turned out to be animal remains. Nothing much exciting goes on 'round here." He frowned.

"Do you have any theories about who it might be?"

"All of us here have theories, luv. Some more than others. Can rule out a well-preserved ancient bog body. Sadly, the estate isn't on a bog. That'd be grand though. Or a Viking."

Neither would have had a 1928 coin on him. I had to be sure not to slip up and give Bernie any of the case's details.

"Could be part of an old undocumented burial ground. That'd be quite the find."

"What about a space alien or British secret agent?"

He chuckled. "Haven't heard either of those. Some wild tales going 'round, aren't there now? Hard to have a proper theory until one has an idea on the age of the bones."

"Did you know the Dunphys?"

He nodded, a reminiscent sparkle in his eyes. "The lads used to give us free sweets. Mostly the eldest one."

"Ernest?"

He shook his head. "No, the other one. Don't recall the fella's name offhand."

Ernest had been the only son listed in the 1911 census. The census was a great resource, but you couldn't assume it included all family members. Older children may have moved away or emigrated, while others were not yet born. Young children in the 1901 census might not be listed with the family in 1911. The child may have died or been living with a widowed aunt helping on the farm. The first child was often born at the mother's family's home in case of complications and to assist the new mother. Mrs. Dunphy's maiden name would be on the couple's civil marriage record. Not only had the eldest likely been born at her parents but may have lived with them or other relations.

Bernie searched stacks of books until he came across a thick hardcover one on the history of Kilcarrigy, written by himself. He paged through the book, coming across a photo for Dunphy's grocer circa 1940. The father and two sons were the same ones in Kiernan's photo album.

"Oscar, that's it." The man pointed out the names noted below the photo. "The eldest lad."

I made a mental note of Ernest's brother.

"The store's now a takeaway place."

Proud of the book he'd authored, the historian had a story for every photo, including several of area cemeteries. Black-and-white photos of Celtic crosses and weathered gravestones in a haze of fog or drizzle captured the mystical setting. I stared mesmerized at the wrought-iron gate leading into Kilcarrigy's cemetery...

"'Tis a lovely graveyard, isn't it?" Bernie said.

I nodded. "I'm obsessed with cemeteries."

"Was the caretaker for several over the years. A brilliant job yet often sad the devastating effect that Mother Nature, neglect, and vandalism can have on gravestones. And not knowing any better, people use harsh chemicals or tools to remove moss and lichen, damaging the stones."

"My grandma and I once spent half my summer vacation removing graffiti from tombstones. I'm heading up a cemetery restoration project in Scotland." I told him about the castle's graveyard. "Many tombstones need repairing. Volunteers will be taught how to clean and care for stones. Many of them date back to the sixteen hundreds. An adopt-a-grave program will encourage Dalwade locals to become involved to make sure the cemetery is taken care of."

Bernie's face lit with enthusiasm. "What a brilliant idea."

"Each volunteer will receive the history of the person buried in the adopted grave. Everyone will fight over Euphemia's grave—the servant who gave Lord Kerr his only male heir. She became his wife after his previous wife mysteriously died. Premium graves like Euphemia's and Lord Kerr's will be tier one at a higher cost. Tier two will include the cemetery's pet section. Hopefully, the area's shelters and humane societies will want to organize volunteers. Part of the donations would go to the organization and part to the hotel."

"Surely locals will jump at the chance to revive such an important landmark. Ya could be enticing them with a few castle perks. Like discounted room rates during the off season."

"That's a great idea. And maybe an annual thank-you reception in the castle's dungeon."

It could be a *costume* reception! I could get at least one more wear out of my tartan gown.

Bernie smiled. "I'd certainly be volunteering if I lived just a bit closer." He winked.

Nearly an hour flew by. Lunch was being served soon, so I decided to head home. I needed to sift through some of the papers from Kiernan before he called and drilled me about what info I'd uncovered. Bernie promised to find more information on the family, and I promised to bring him more books when I returned. I left with an optimistic outlook that somewhere in the man's personal archives was an important clue that the historian was going to discover.

As I walked toward the entrance, Biddy texted.

The eejit's post has 5,000 likes and 147 shares!

My grip tightened on the phone. The more people who saw the post, the more likely we'd be identified.

Elvis Presley's "Rock-a-Hula Baby" playing in a resident's room eased my tension. Grandma's favorite Elvis movie, *Blue Hawaii*. I smiled at the memories of having watched it with her a dozen times. I peeked through the room's open door. A short plump woman in a purple floral pant set and white tennies was swaying her hips to the catchy tune while slowly shuffling her feet sideways across the tile floor.

She smiled and waved me in. "Come in, luv. Don't be shy."

"Sorry. Didn't mean to be nosey."

"Not a' tall, luv. Join me. A hula a day keeps the doctor away, ya know."

It seemed to be working. The woman had to be at least ninety. At her insistence, I swayed my hips back and forth, making a lilting motion with my hands. On TV, Elvis was entertaining guests at his overbearing mother's dinner party. Dressed in a white jacket and black slacks, he gyrated his hips to the beat of his Hawaiian-attired band playing the bongos and maraca-like shakers. The song ended, and the woman muted the volume.

"Ah, that was grand, wasn't it now? Never gets old, it doesn't. Dance to it every day." She eased down into a rose-colored upholstered chair and gestured for me to sit in the matching one across from her. She introduced herself as Julia.

"Was my grandma's favorite Elvis movie," I said.

"Good for putting a bit of bounce in our step on a dreary day."

Framed prints of Hawaii and other tropical locales hung on the yellow walls.

"Have you been to Hawaii?"

"No, luv. Once went to the Canary Islands, and Florida a few times to visit me son and his family."

"My dad lives in Florida."

She smiled. "Knew you weren't an Irish lass. A blow-in from Florida, are ya?"

I shook my head. "Chicago, but I inherited my grandma's cottage over in Ballycaffey last year. My mom grew up in Ireland."

"Ah, Ballycaffey. Lovely place." She gave me a sympathetic smile. "Sorry to hear about your granny."

"Thanks. Are you from the area?"

"Born in Kilcarrigy."

"So, you must have a theory on the skeleton."

She shrugged. "I'm thinking it was before the Dunphy family lived there. Didn't seem like the type of people who'd bury a body in their yard and carry on as if nothing had happened."

"You knew the Dunphys?"

She nodded. "The young Mrs. Dunphy worked for a bit in the grocery store. Nice lady. Wasn't too sure about her husband though. Was a bit of a cad."

"Ernest?"

Her gaze narrowed. "No, not the Dunphy fella. The lad before him. Was a different name one doesn't often hear in Ireland. Gilroy, Gibby..."

"Gilbert?"

She snapped her fingers. "Why yes, Gilbert. Nice-looking fella but a bit dodgy. Had a crush on me friend Annie. Was always offering to buy her sweets or an ice cream. Of course, she'd never have accepted such gifts from a married man." Smiling, she gazed out the window, her eyelids heavy. "Ah, Annie..."

She drifted off. I draped a green knit blanket over the woman's lap. Had Gilbert Moffat, Isobel's first husband, been trying to be a nice guy by offering Annie sweets and his gesture was mistaken for crude behavior? Or had he been a womanizer?

I walked out the door and nearly ran over a petite wisp of a woman wearing a pink dress with a full pleated skirt and pale pink ballet slippers. Her white hair was up in a loose bun. Pink blush and pink lipstick added color to her porcelain skin. The elegant woman reminded me of Rosie in another ten years.

"Heard ya was calling in on Bernie McBride about the Dunphys." She quirked a curious brow. "From the newspaper, are ya?"

"No, was just paying him a visit."

She nodded skeptically.

"Why? Do you have a theory?" I asked.

Along with the other fifty residents here.

A mysterious glint sparkled in her pale-blue eyes. "I best be off to lunch. It's Italian today. If I'm late, the garlic sticks will all be gone." She walked off, stepping softly against the tiled floor.

When I reached my car, I glanced back at the home to find the ballet-slipper woman peering out a window at me, then she disappeared. I'd have to pay her a visit on my next trip here. I'd bring Biddy with me to help make the rounds. We'd have to stay focused on the task at hand and limit each visit to fifteen minutes. Like speed dating, except without the awkward conversation, anxiety, and alcohol.

Nine

I TOSSED a handful of Froot Loops out the kitchen window, and Pinky scarfed them up. I scarfed down my second bowl of cereal, needing comfort food, since I'd polished off the baked pumpkin seeds. That stupid Twitter photo of Biddy and me and the skeletonscavenger and graverobber hashtags were haunting me. My trip to the nursing home hadn't been overly productive. And I was bummed I hadn't heard from Gretta. The minute she knew anything, I'd know. I had heard from Kiernan Moffat twice, demanding a status report. I'd responded that I was sorting through loads of clues. Hopefully, Edmond and Rosie had uncovered some great ones that would get the guy off my back.

I located Ernest Dunphy's parents' marriage record and learned his mother's maiden name. I found their eldest son, Oscar, living with her parents in a nearby village. Interesting. Why hadn't he lived with his family in Kilcarrigy?

I sorted through the records from the Dunphys' floor safe. The papers included the estate's land records, Ernest's and his father's wills, and business records pertaining to their grocery store, including another ledger.

The father's will mentioned Oscar, Ernest, and two sisters. That made four children, the same as what was in the family photos. When the father died in 1946, Oscar had inherited the home and several acres of land. The remaining acres were divided between Ernest and his two sisters, one married and one unmarried. The two sons split the grocery business. Two brothers co-owning a business could have been a family feud waiting to happen.

According to the land records, in 1898 the Dunphys had acquired the property from an English landlord. What a celebration that must have been. Fiddle music played in my head, accompanied by visions of couples dancing through the night. The festivities might have gone on for days. What a triumphant time, owning their own land for the first time in generations and not paying rent to farm it. As a bonus, they'd then had a spot to bury a body twenty-some years later.

The doorbell rang.

I let Biddy in along with the scent of Kung Pao chicken. My favorite.

"Over nine thousand likes and two hundred thirty shares." She announced our current stats before I could cover my ears.

I poured two glasses of red wine and returned to the living room with the bottle and glasses.

"I'm tracking down this Gaelic Gobshite fella in case we need to pay him a visit."

"Why would we want to do that?" I took a gulp of wine.

"If the fella's post goes viral, he won't make money from

Twitter, but he could make loads off it in other ways. We might be wanting to hunt him down and demand our share."

"Not if he hasn't identified us."

"Also can't be suing him without his address. Anyway, his profile name is Gaelic Galway Guy, and it appears he actually lives in Galway. Half the places he follows are on the north side of the city. And—"

"I think you could be putting your social media damage control time to better use."

"Didn't take me over fifteen minutes to figure it out." She topped off her wine. "How was your day?"

I recounted my research while we devoured the takeaway.

"I wasn't super productive," I said.

Biddy relaxed back on the couch with her second glass of wine. "Having pieced together Ernest Dunphy's family is a major accomplishment. And maybe those surrounding gravestone snaps will be other rellies who are missing a family member because he was buried under the shed and not in the family plot."

"I also heard a rumor that Gilbert Moffat might have been a bit of a ladies' man."

"Always grand to pick up some juicy gossip on the side."

"We really need a solid lead."

"A lead on my car would also be brill. Garda Higgins finally returned my message. Seeing as it's part of an investigation, he said he's not at liberty to disclose its location. How mad is that? As if I don't have the right to know where my car is at. Told him it better at least be getting a proper washing and that an oil change would be grand since I've been so bloody accommodating. Seriously? How long does it take to figure out if there are any bones under my car?" Biddy took a gulp of wine, her cheeks flaming.

"As if two days without a car is anything compared to poor Skelly having been in the ground for who knows how many years."

Biddy shrugged. "Sorry. Just worried they haven't a clue where my car is and are trying to figure out how to break the news to me. You're always hearing about evidence going missing."

"A car would be an awfully big thing to lose."

The doorbell rang.

I dragged myself off the couch and greeted Edmond and Rosie. The red-eyed, exhausted couple nearly collapsed on the love seat while I poured Edmond a whiskey and Rosie a glass of wine. Not being a whiskey drinker, I kept the bottle on hand for guests. The Murray tartan–labeled Scotch on the white kitchen countertop was a souvenir from my family reunion. I'd had a swig during a desperate moment in Scotland when Ava had dropped the bomb that she thought her nasty brother Malcolm was my father. Thankfully, she'd been wrong.

Another reason I should appreciate the fact that Ian was my biological father.

I served the drinks and biscuits, then sat on the couch with Biddy. The couple went right for the alcohol.

"You two look wrecked," Biddy said. "Maybe you should cut back on the number of hours you're spending at the library."

I nodded. "You're at least taking a lunch break, I hope."

"If we aren't there from opening to closing, we'll never get the case solved." The wrinkles around Rosie's eyes deepened. "It takes nearly all day for one of us to view a half year of newspapers. Thankfully, they hadn't been printed daily. Fifty-two papers are plenty."

Edmond nodded. "Rosie started with the 1928 papers, and I began with 1933. Thought it might be a good idea to spread the research out."

"Could go a bit faster but would hate to miss something of importance." Rosie nibbled on her bottom lip.

"No worries. Take your time," I said. "I appreciate your help." A perfect segue into telling them I'd recruited Gretta. I didn't want them being offended that I was bringing in reinforcements, as if I doubted their ability to complete the task. "Last night Gretta came into the pub and offered to assist. I thought it'd be crazy to turn down her help since there are decades of papers. She's starting with 1940 and reviewing forward. She's using my account for the historical newspaper site."

Rosie washed down the news with a large gulp of wine, then managed an uneasy smile rather than her usual pleasant one. "More help is always nice."

Edmond nodded. "Indeed."

Rosie took another drink of wine. "Indeed," she muttered.

"I hope that's okay."

"Of course, luv," Edmond said. "Makes perfect sense, it does."

Rosie smiled. "Yes, the woman is quite...driven. She'll be grand."

A polite way of saying Gretta was strong-willed and competitive, even though she'd turned over a new leaf in many respects. The reason she and Biddy often butted heads

—they shared several similar traits. Whereas Rosie and Gretta couldn't have been more opposite.

Biddy peered anxiously at the couple. "So did ya uncover any clues today?"

A smile lit Rosie's face. "My, yes. A bit about Mary Kelly, a hoity-toity girl I worked with at a shop when I first moved to the area. Seems her parents were repeatedly charged with serving watered-downed whiskey in their pub. They'd grown the family business by cheating friends and neighbors. Likely why they had to move here and start a new business where nobody knew them."

"Wonder if I could be getting dirt on that wretched Hannah Riley at work," Biddy mused.

"We also found several bits that might be of help to your investigation," Edmond said.

Rosie handed me a stack of papers from her tote. The top one advertised the Dunphys' store. "Loads of large ads for the family's grocery store prominently placed in the paper. The establishment was apparently doing quite well. Not sure if they'll provide any clues but thought I should copy just in case."

I nodded. "Absolutely. Anything could be a clue."

Rosie smiled lovingly at her boyfriend. "Edmond hit the jackpot."

The man plucked a pair of wire glasses from his shirt pocket and slipped them on. "Came across an interesting court record in 1933." He removed a sheet of paper from his folder. The article's headline read: "Falling Out at Kilcarrigy, Between Prominent Shopkeeper and Supplier." "A local farmer, James Sheehan, supplied rashers and pork to the store and wasn't paid the agreed-upon price for them. Dispute was between the fella and an Oscar Dunphy."

"Oscar was the oldest son," I said.

Edmond handed me another article. "The following week in a petty session incident, the Sheehan fella was fined for starting a row with Oscar Dunphy in the middle of town. The court saw in favor of Mr. Dunphy in both instances."

"A fight gone bad, and the farmer ended up buried under the shed?" Biddy said.

"That's easy enough to verify if a death record is on file," I said. "Now we know that Oscar Dunphy might have been lacking work ethics, if the plaintiff's claim was true."

Had the Dunphys made their money by cheating local farmers of their hard-earned money? Like Rosie's hoity-toity coworker's family pub?

"Everyone I've talked to so far seemed to have liked the Dunphys," I said.

"No mention of the farmer having mysteriously disappeared in the following months." Rosie shook her head in disappointment. "Not one missing person so far. Several cattle and sheep went missing more often than one would think. Over fifty sheep one time. Luckily, the next week's paper announced they'd found the thief, who was up on charges."

"Could be the person buried there wasn't a local," I said. "Keep an eye out for mention of any relations or out-of-town guests visiting the Dunphys."

The couple finished their drinks, and I wished them a good night and suggested they take it easier the next day. Biddy followed them out, and we made plans to visit the Kilcarrigy nursing home tomorrow.

I enjoyed the quiet house and another glass of wine while locating the death record for the pig farmer who'd filed charges against Oscar. That confirmed the man wasn't Skelly. Our potential-victims list remained at zero. So did our chances of a *Roadshow* episode set at Dalwade Castle Hotel and Spa unless I added names to the list ASAP.

Ten

THE FOLLOWING MORNING, I was on the couch sipping a cup of tea, avoiding the urge to check the status of our skeleton scavenger photo on Twitter. Had we officially gone viral? I tried to remain optimistic that Biddy and I had successfully diverted the negative media attention from Kiernan Moffat. And no way were people going to identify us. This would turn out to be a positive situation. However, it probably wasn't a good idea to mention it to the appraiser, who might not see the upside of another photo drawing attention to the estate and Skelly.

I'd been unable to resist checking email several times for a response from Ian. Nothing. It'd been twenty-four hours since I'd emailed him. Had my involvement with Skelly freaked him out? Rather than being neurotic over not emailing him, now I could be neurotic over him not responding.

The doorbell rang. Typically Biddy wouldn't stop over at 7:30 a.m. on her day off. She'd likely never gone to bed, up watching our Twitter pic go viral. It turned out to be Gretta.

She zipped inside along with the scent of coffee, steam rising from the to-go cup in her hand.

"Had to go into town. Out of coffee. Thought I'd drop off what I found a few hours ago." Wired on caffeine, she'd likely pulled an all-nighter. "After searching two years of papers, I came across a juicy bit in April 1941. Not sure it'll mean much for the case, but it's interesting." She handed me a copy of the article. "Sorry it's not clearer. My printer is banjaxed. My son ordered me a new one. Should be here soon, hopefully. Anyway, it's about a court appearance. Seems a woman's husband stormed into the Moffats' residence accusing Gilbert Moffat of making suggestive advances toward his wife. It notes the man's name, not his wife's. Gilbert denied it and in turn filed a charge against the fella for sullying his good name and using foul and abusive language in front of his family."

No surprise Gretta had come across a court record same as Edmond. Half the newspapers content at that time included court cases with detailed transcripts for nosey neighbors' reading enjoyment.

"Gilbert Moffat won the case," she said.

That didn't mean he'd been innocent.

"I best be getting back to it. Will be in touch." As Gretta headed out the door, she turned to me and smiled. "And thanks a million. Both for assisting with my DNA test and occupying my time so that's not the only thing I'm thinking about."

"You're welcome."

A nervous feeling fluttered in my chest in anticipation of the woman's test results. I wasn't sure I was emotionally up to dealing with Gretta's DNA discoveries over the holidays.

I sat at the kitchen table and read the article on Gilbert Moffat. This information, along with Julia—the woman at the nursing home—calling Gilbert a cad, put Isobel's second husband in a better light than her first. It didn't appear the war hero had been a stand-up guy when it came to his personal life. Curious, I decided to do a bit of research on the man. My current profile on him merely noted his death date, his wife, and his three children, including Kiernan's father.

An hour later I'd searched several online databases listing UK prisoners of war, WWII British casualties, war graves, and others. I came up empty. Even more interesting, there were no records for Gilbert having been drafted or enlisted. As a Scottish citizen, I assumed the UK military could have drafted him.

How could a man who'd never enlisted, fought, or died in a war have received a medal? To confirm Gilbert was the legit recipient of Kiernan's medal, I'd have to write to an armed services department. I didn't doubt the authenticity of the medal as much as I doubted that Gilbert Moffat was on that list.

How had Kiernan obtained a medal for a man who was never in the war? Fake war medals sounded like something the appraiser would be involved in. However, he wouldn't have showcased a forgery on TV and connected it to his family. Maybe like father, like son—his dad had made the medal or found it in an antique shop. Or his grandmother had. Either way, if one of them had known Gilbert hadn't been awarded a medal, the person had likely known about the man's possible fake death.

Who would have fabricated such a detailed military hero story? More than the *who*, I was interested in the *why*.

What reason would someone have had for claiming Gilbert Moffat was killed in the war?

Because he was killed and buried under the garden shed?

Fed up with her husband's philandering and her public humiliation, had Isobel clobbered him over the head with a shovel? But why would he have been buried under the shed? She hadn't married Ernest until years after her husband was supposedly killed during the war in 1944.

Maybe Isobel's husband hadn't been the only unfaithful one in their marriage. Maybe she'd been seeing Ernest on the side. A wealthy and respectable businessman compared to her cheating jerk of a husband.

What if Ernest and Isobel were in on the murder together?

Stop jumping to conclusions.

Maybe there was a reason I hadn't been able to find Gilbert Moffat's military records. Maybe Gilbert was a nick-name or his middle name, not his legal name. Or his army records went missing because of a filing snafu or on purpose because he'd been killed while on a covert mission for army intelligence. It would have been top secret, so his file wouldn't be available to the public on genealogy sites. That was the least plausible scenario from the little I'd learned about the unheroic and immoral man's character. Unless he'd been a *double* agent.

Hopefully, Kiernan could provide a logical explanation for his grandfather's missing military records.

I didn't invite Biddy to tag along on my visit to see Kiernan Moffat. Not only did she need to be troubleshooting social media—outside of our photo—I feared what might be disturbing news about the man's grandfather Gilbert was best delivered one on one. He might be more rational and open to discussing it without Biddy saying the wrong thing and setting him off.

Upon arriving at the estate, I received a text from Biddy.

Over 20,000 likes and 421 shares. Going to hunt down the bloody eejit and...

I closed her text, wanting to maintain a positive attitude for my conversation with Kiernan rather than hear about Biddy's horrific plans for Gaelic Gobshite. After a few calming breaths, I walked across the dried parking area to the house.

Kiernan answered the door wearing a crisply pressed blue oxford and tan slacks. The mingling scents of spearmint gum, musky aftershave, and almond-scented hair products, rather than whiskey, were a good sign. It appeared he'd taken several steps back from the edge he'd been teetering on two days ago.

I feared that was about to change.

"Haven't heard more from the garda," he said, heading up the stairs to the library. "Can't imagine they could have anything worse to tell me. I certainly hope you're here to deliver good news. Discovered the man's identity, have you?" He poured me a cup of tea from a fancy French tea press on the credenza.

I managed a faint smile. "Working on piecing everything together. Finished sorting through the papers from the safe and the ones you gave me. I thought I'd possibly come across your grandfather Gilbert's military papers."

He shrugged. "My grandmother might never have had the papers."

"So...she didn't pass down any of your grandpa's other military things?"

He shook his head. "Merely the medal. What could be more significant than that?"

"You'd think the medal would have come with a certificate."

"Quite possible it had." He slowly lowered the teacup from his lips. "Are you questioning the medal's authenticity?"

Along with your grandfather's.

"As if I'd try to pass off a fake war medal as my grandfather's, giving the illusion he was a military hero?"

"Not on purpose."

He blew an impatient puff of air between his lips, glancing down at his watch. "Please get on with whatever it is you're trying to accuse me of. After our discussion, I decided I indeed need to return to work despite the producer's insistence otherwise. Refuse to have that nitwit appraiser-wannabe killing the show's ratings. The idiot dresses like a clown. Doesn't even wear a watch. By the way, ratings are soaring thanks to the Halloween episode, despite all the challenges." He glanced at his watch once again. "I must be off."

"I don't think your grandfather was killed in the war," I blurted out. "Or that he was ever in the war. He's not listed in any UK military or war databases. There's no record of him having enlisted or being drafted. How could he have received a medal if he'd never enlisted, fought, or died in the war?"

Kiernan shrugged off my theory. "Apparently the databases aren't inclusive of all records." He eyed the crystal whiskey decanter on the cart across the room. "There's certainly a logical explanation. Where on earth would my grandmother have obtained a war medal pre-eBay and internet? And why would she have fabricated such an elaborate story?"

The man followed my gaze to the window overlooking the crime scene tape below.

"Gone completely mad, have you?" He slammed his delicate teacup down, rattling its saucer on the credenza.

"It's just a theory."

"And a bloody awful one. Besides the fact that my dear grandmother never could have killed a rat, I just bragged to the entire world about my war-hero grandfather."

"Wouldn't you rather know the truth?"

He bolted to the liquor cart, then decided against it. He had to drive to Dublin. If he still ended up going after our discussion.

"What if I'm right?" My tone was sympathetic and rational.

"You're not!"

"But what if I *am* and someone who knows the truth saw the episode and disputes your claim and military heirloom? Or a nosey military expert reviews the recipient list and discovers your grandfather isn't on it?"

Panic filled the man's blue eyes. He snagged a Cuban cigar from the antique humidor on the desk. He clipped the end and lit it. I took several steps back, my nose crinkling in protest at the pungent stench of the hundred-dollar cigar.

"You don't want to be blindsided, do you?" I threw open the window, breathing in the fresh air. "If the garda pursue a criminal investigation, you might be required to provide a DNA sample."

He tugged his tie loose and undid his shirt's top button. He took a deep drag on his cigar.

"You'd have had no way of knowing. You're an antique book appraiser, not an expert on military collectibles. You'd never have felt the need to have the medal authenticated when it was a family heirloom. And you'd certainly never planned to sell it."

A week ago I wouldn't have questioned the possibility of the guy selling his family heirloom. Having now seen how passionate he was about the medal, he wouldn't have sold it.

"Stop trying to make me feel better. And stop your research! I can no longer afford your fee."

"You're not paying me."

"Then stop or the Dalwade filming is off."

"We have a contract."

"My lawyer could rip that to shreds in a matter of seconds. Null and void."

Heart racing, I reined in the anger raging inside me. "You need to learn the truth before anyone else does. There's at least a fifty percent chance my hunch isn't right."

He paled. "A *fifty* percent chance it *is*?"

Was the guy more worried about his reputation or his grandma having killed and buried his grandpa under the garden shed?

"I can't drop this." I squared my shoulders and stared

him straight in the eyes. "If you don't care to uncover the truth, I owe it to the victim. Remember when I didn't want you moving forward with the mourning jewelry episode because I thought I came from a family of felons? Shoe is on the other foot now. Yet if I discover Skelly's your grandfather, I won't threaten to air it on TV. I respect your privacy, which is why I came alone today. But I have an ethical obligation to pursue this."

"If you do, the Dalwade Castle episode is off." He swiped a hand through the air.

My breathing quickened, my hands balled into fists at my side. "So if I don't pursue the victim's identity and keep my mouth shut, you'll keep up your end of the bargain to film at the castle? That's like blackmail, extortion, or something unethical. Which is low even for you."

Rather than looking offended, he wore a smug smile. "That's the deal. Take it or leave it."

"I'll leave it," I snapped. "Maybe I'll come up with a bit of blackmail evidence myself that'll make you change your mind about filming at the castle."

Heart going berserk, I turned and stalked out, mortified that I'd just sunk to the appraiser's level.

For the *second* time!

Eleven

I WAS NO BETTER than Kiernan Moffat, resorting to threats and underhanded tactics. Could I have acted more unprofessional when I should have shown compassion for the guy after the bomb I'd just dropped? Had *I* discovered that Grandma had buried Grandpa in my backyard, I'd have gone off the deep end. However, Kiernan had backed me into a corner, threatening me first, putting me on the defense. At least I hadn't mentioned the adultery charge filed against his grandpa Gilbert or Julia's story about him hitting on her young friend Annie.

If I stopped researching poor Skelly's identity, *Rags to Riches Roadshow* would film at Dalwade Castle. If I continued, the filming was off unless I resorted to blackmail. I should have lied and claimed the castle's owner had already launched a marketing campaign about the hotel's upcoming appearance on the show. It would have looked bad for Kiernan and the show to have canceled at that point.

Nevertheless, I had an ethical obligation to pursue my hunch. Hopefully, my hunch was wrong, and Kiernan would be so ecstatic he'd forget my threat and the filming would be a go.

If I couldn't prove Gilbert Moffat *was* the skeleton, I had to prove he *wasn't*.

What else could have happened to the man, who'd supposedly died in the war? What horrible thing would have caused Isobel to have claimed he was dead?

Because she'd *wished* the no-good cheating jerk was dead?

If he hadn't gone off to war, had he gone off with another woman and abandoned his family?

Regardless of the actual circumstances, Gilbert Moffat had to have died *somewhere*.

I found two small family trees online belonging to descendants of Gilbert's older brother. Trees often contained incorrect information, so I needed to verify if the person had indeed been Gilbert's brother, along with two other siblings. The only information on Gilbert was his birth date. Forget about Kiernan sharing family background. I'd conduct my own research for Gilbert and Isobel Moffat, including extended family. Hiding out with a distant relative was a definite possibility. I needed every obit and historical record for his family members. Who knew where he might pop up?

Luckily, Gilbert Moffat would have been an uncommon name in Ireland and Northern Ireland. Gilbert likely hadn't been a popular name in Scotland either. Fingers crossed I wouldn't have to expand my research to Australia, the States, or Biddy's dream hut on a remote South Pacific island.

Ireland's civil records index didn't list a Gilbert Moffat, so either he'd died after 1970 or outside of the country. According to Northern Ireland's and Scotland's available records, he hadn't died in either of those countries. None of the major cemetery research sites listed a Gilbert Moffat matching Kiernan's grandpa buried in one of the three countries or any other countries. Volunteers contributed the information, so it was hit or miss if a grave was listed.

Had Gilbert remained in Ireland or fled to Scotland, his Moffats' homeland? If he'd had relations in Scotland, they'd likely known about his family and would have discovered he'd deserted them. Also, it would have been one of the first places his wife would have searched for him, had she cared to find him.

Yet Isobel would have been better off *not* having found Gilbert. She undoubtedly hadn't wanted the jerk to return home, and in Ireland at that time, an abandoned spouse wasn't allowed to remarry. Unlike in the US, where most States had permitted divorce on the grounds of abandonment, adultery, and abuse. Ireland hadn't legalized divorce until a 1995 referendum by a very slim margin. This was another valid reason for Isobel having fabricated the story about her husband's death.

She'd be free to marry Ernest Dunphy.

Had Gilbert also made up a tale about his spouse's supposed death, enabling him to remarry? Or had he claimed he'd never been married? A local records office or priest might not have taken the initiative and verified Gilbert's marital status or his first wife's death. There wouldn't have been a central records database, and much of rural Ireland hadn't had phone service. I checked all three countries, and the only marriage records listed for a Gilbert Moffat was the one for Gilbert and Isobel and for a man thirty years prior to that in Donegal. Possibly his second marriage had occurred less than seventy-five years ago, so the privacy law prevented its inclusion online.

If he ran off with a local woman, her family would surely have known, or she'd have been reported as missing. Not only should my research team be looking for missing *men* in the paper but also missing *women*. Since Gretta was researching the 1940s papers, I left her a message to expand her search to include missing females. I instructed her to work backward from 1944, when Gilbert had supposedly been killed in the war.

A quick search confirmed that the man in the paper who'd filed adultery charges against Gilbert was buried with his wife in the Kilcarrigy cemetery. His wife's name wasn't Annie, the friend of Julia. Perhaps Annie had been more interested in the married man than Julia had thought, but their liaison had remained a secret. I needed to pay Julia another visit.

Elvis's "Rock-a-Hula Baby" played in my head while I grabbed several genealogy books from my office for the local historian, Bernie McBride. I'd have to stop and buy a gift for Julia. I was also anxious to visit the mysterious woman in the ballet slippers. I headed to McCarthy's to pick up my wingman, Biddy. Between the two of us we should be able to get a few dozen theories as to Skelly's identity. Even if the stories were tall tales, genealogy research had taught me that incorrect information on historical records often held a thread of truth.

For example, I hadn't known Delia was a nickname for Bridget. I'd once assumed a death certificate was way off noting the mother's name as Delia Grieves instead of Bridget Connolly. When I learned Delia was a nickname, I started questioning the last name Grieves. Rather than an error, maybe it had been the maiden name of that woman's mother or grandmother. The mystery remained unsolved, but I'd learned an important genealogy lesson.

I entered the pub, where Ita stood behind the bar massaging her temples while Biddy sat chatting with Johnny, dressed in a *Fear the Deere* tractor T-shirt.

"He has another theory about the skeleton found over in Kilcarrigy," Biddy told me.

"Not merely a theory, it isn't," the man said. "'Tis what happened, without a doubt."

Ita placed a bag of Taytos on the bar. "You're going to need them." She gave me a wink.

I opened the bag and popped several onion-and-cheese-flavored chips into my mouth.

"Was talking to me friend down near Kilcarrigy," Johnny said. "His family owned the pub next to Dunphy's grocer. Had a sort of bed-and-breakfast above it. If fellas had a few too many jars, the owner would give 'em a fifty percent discount on an available room. A brilliant plan. Place was sure to sell out every evening." He glanced over at Ita stocking the beer fridge. "Should be thinking about giving it a try, ya should."

"Think I take enough care of you all during the day. Don't need to be tucking you in at night."

"I'm sorry—what does that theory have to do with the skeleton?" I asked impatiently.

"That's not the theory, lass." He took a drink of beer. "A dodgy fella would rent a room each month when conducting business with the Dunphys' store. What sort of business is the question." He waggled his brows in a mysterious manner. "He was once in town when the store had a break-in. One of the Dunphy lads was messed up something fierce. So bad he ended up at a Dublin A and E and was in the hospital for weeks."

"Ernest Dunphy?" I asked.

"Haven't a clue which fella."

"You think that dodgy salesman was caught breaking in, killed, then buried in the Dunphys' yard?" I asked.

Biddy eyes widened. "My random robbery theory..."

He shrugged. "Why else would he have been leaving town without his suitcase?"

Biddy and I exchanged intrigued glances.

This theory was more plausible than his one about the annoying tea and tomato salesman.

"A few days later, me friend's mum called in on the Dunphys, inquiring on how she might reach the fella about his suitcase. Had no phone number or address for the man. Old Mrs. Dunphy said she hadn't a clue and had enough to worry about with her son being in a Dublin hospital."

"Who'd have buried the dead salesman if the brother was in the hospital?" Biddy asked.

He shrugged. "Supposing the other brother or father."

"Do you know when this happened?" I asked.

"Before the 1950s. Me friend was merely a wee lad. If you'd like, I could be asking him."

"Actually, I'd love to buy you both a pint if he'd care to stop by and tell me anything else he knows."

I might end up forgiving Johnny for the Tombstone Terminator nickname. It was a term of endearment compared to Body Snatcher and Skeleton Scavenger.

He smiled wide. "Will be bringing him 'round tomorrow."

I added the dodgy suitcase salesman to my list of possible victims. Even though the story had likely been embellished over the years, or over a few pints between Johnny and his friend, I liked it better than mine.

Unfortunately, I feared Gilbert Moffat was Skelly.

Johnny went over to play darts with a buddy.

"How's the investigation going?" Ita asked.

I told her and Biddy about my theory that Gilbert Moffat hadn't gone off to war but somewhere else. I saved the part about Kiernan's threat to cancel the castle episode for the drive, or Biddy would lose it and the entire bar would become privy to our *secret* investigation.

"If Isobel made up the story because her husband abandoned the family for another woman, why not have him die a painful death?" Biddy said. "Why in the world make him a war hero?"

I nodded. "Right? Have him eaten by sharks or a rabid pack of wolves."

"A slower, more painful death would have been better. Same for that nasty Gaelic Gobshite fella. Like getting attacked by a swarm of bees when being allergic to them, then living in agony until his head swelled up so big it exploded. Or having stepped on a red ant hill and having them crawl up his legs into his knickers and—"

"Jaysus," Collin said, walking up behind us. "When I agreed to be helping you bury a body one day, I didn't know you were already making plans." He grimaced.

Biddy smiled at her boyfriend—a cute brown-haired guy

dressed in jeans and a lightweight blue sweater that brought out the blue in his eyes. "I like to be prepared."

"Maybe I should be having second thoughts about us going away together on holiday." He draped an arm around her shoulders. "Even if just for the weekend."

Biddy and Collin were going away together for a weekend?

She ignored my curious stare. "Can only be going if Mags and I identify Skelly."

Their getaway was apparently soon, yet Biddy hadn't mentioned it.

"Wicklow should be lovely with the autumn leaves on the trees," Ita said.

Biddy's *mom* knew their plans when I hadn't a clue?

Hmm... Was this payback for me not telling Biddy what was wrong with Gretta? Or because I hadn't been open to discussing Ian, only because I didn't know what to discuss.

"What do you guys plan to do?" I asked.

Collin shot a surprised glance from Biddy to me. "Biddy didn't be telling ya? Talked her into a ghost tour at Wicklow Gaol. At night."

I eyed Biddy. "You're doing a haunted prison tour?"

She shifted on her stool. "After our ghost tour in Edinburgh, I'm a bit mad for haunted places."

Collin smiled. "And going hiking at Ballinastoe."

"It's not hiking, more of a walk," Biddy assured me since she'd never hiked in her life. "The Devil's Glen walk. Supposed to be gorgeous."

"Ah, it's lovely," Ita said. "A lass at work had snaps of it this past summer. Her boyfriend proposed on the walk."

Biddy paled. Her smile faded.

Collin glanced at his watch, missing her reaction. "Lunch is over. I best be getting back to work." He gave Biddy a fleeting kiss and was off.

Before I could interrogate Biddy, she sprang from her chair. "Must craic on ourselves. Lots to do." She whisked out the door to my car.

Our drive to Kilcarrigy was going to be a tense one.

Twelve

"No filming at Dalwade?" Biddy fumed in the seat next to me. "He won't be getting away with this. He signed a contract. We'll hire a solicitor. We'll sue!"

Biddy's reaction was precisely why I hadn't had her join me on my visit with the appraiser. I'd been irrational enough.

"We're not suing Kiernan. The guy wasn't thinking clearly. I'd just told him his grandma might have murdered his grandpa and buried him under her garden shed."

"Not like the cheating jerk hadn't deserved it."

"Regardless, it's a horrible thing to learn about your grandparents. And having bragged about his war-hero grandfather to millions just adds salt to the wound."

Biddy dropped back against the car seat. "Suppose. But he shouldn't be taking it out on the castle or us. Especially when he's best off knowing the truth before others find out. Speaking of which, I still haven't been tagged in that Gaelic Gobshite's post. We remain the unidentified skeleton scavengers." She checked her Twitter account. "Over thirty thousand likes and six hundred shares."

"I think you need a social media time-out."

I certainly did.

She tossed her phone into her purse. "When are the guards going to decide if there'll be an investigation?"

I shrugged. "No clue."

We pulled into the nursing home lot. I grabbed the bag of books from the back along with a pink gift bag. We'd stopped at a shop and bought Julia some fancy coconut-scented lotion and bath gel. Now she could be immersed in the tropical scent of Hawaii.

"Remember, fifteen minutes max for each visit," I said. "Stay focused on our purpose for being here."

"A bit rigid when we're likely the highlight of these people's day."

"I get it, but I spent an hour and a half chatting with the local historian about area cemeteries and my restoration project and not about the Dunphys. It was quite interesting, just not the background we need." I peered at the home. "And everyone here surely has a theory on Skelly. Think of the wealth of historical information within those walls. It'll all be gone when the residents pass away, unless someone like Bernie McBride has recorded it."

"You need to be finishing your granny's school journal."

Grandma had a hardcover journal with handwritten stories from former students who'd returned years later to visit her home, the old Ballycaffey National School. At bedtime Grandma would read me journal entries rather than fairy tales. Sadly, she'd never thought to add her own stories to the journal. I'd been carrying the tales around in my head for years and began documenting them after her death.

I nodded. "I should make a copy for the library's history room."

"Better yet, publish it and give copies to attendees at the school reunion next summer. A memento they could pass down to their children." Biddy's eyes widened. "A family heirloom. A hundred years from now, some genealogist might discover it while searching through the books in the library's history room. Publishing your own book is easy. My auntie Violet published one about Irish moss. Did you know there are over a thousand types of moss here?"

My only interest in moss was preventing it from destroying fragile gravestones beyond repair.

I added the book idea to my mile-long to-do list.

The same woman who'd buzzed me in the other day was there, so Bernie didn't have to meet me at the front door and parade me through the halls. Lunch had recently ended, a group of women were making floral arrangements, and several residents were in the common room off the foyer, where *Father Ted* was blaring on the TV. Biddy went into the room to visit while I walked down the hall toward the historian's room. I found the man snoring away in the recliner by the window, sunshine and a red knitted throw blanket keeping him warm. Disappointed I wouldn't be able to see if he'd found any further details on the Dunphys in his history collection, I set the bag of books on his bed. The only area free of books and papers besides the floor. I wrote a note that I'd pop in again soon to chat.

I rapped on Julia's open door and peeked in at the woman watching Elvis and Ann-Margret in *Viva Las Vegas*.

She smiled wide and waved me in. "Ah, so glad you called

in for another visit, luv." She muted the TV's volume. "Felt awful having fallen asleep during our talk the other day."

"No worries, I had to be leaving anyway. But I'd love to hear more about your friend Annie."

"Ah, yes, Annie Fallon."

I handed her the small pink gift bag.

"Ya shouldn't have, luv. But thanks a million." She gave me a wink. We rubbed the silky, coconut-scented lotion on our hands. She closed her eyes, taking a deep breath. "Just like being on a tropical beach."

I sniffed my hands while peering out at the drizzle.

"We were great friends, Annie and me." Julia's smile faded. "At least I'd thought we were. Had planned to rent a flat together in Dublin after receiving our school certificates. Were going to work at Clery's department store on O'Connell Street. To think, the store is still there today. At least I believe it is."

I nodded. "Bought a sweater there this past spring."

"Instead, I married a publican and bought a home just up the way from me family's farm. Mickey and I had three fine lads and a lovely life. Just always wonder what it would have been like to be a city lass even just for a wee bit."

"I was born and raised in Chicago. Personally, I'm much happier here in my rural cottage, even though Dublin is a lovely city. Why didn't you and Annie move there?"

"In the summer of 1943, a year before finishing our schooling, she went to stay with relations in the States. Quite a sudden decision. One night she called in to say goodbye and was gone the next. An ill aunt in New York had needed minding. She'd promised to send me her address...but never did." She frowned. "Was supposed to have been merely a temporary stay."

If Biddy ever ran off with Collin and never contacted me, I'd hunt her down. Besides the fact that she knew I had the skills to find her, she'd never abandon me. Except for a holiday weekend with Collin in Wicklow. Biddy had spent the entire drive here wiggin' out over Kiernan threatening to cancel the filming. I hadn't had a chance to ask about her weekend getaway.

Why had Annie abandoned her best friend and their exciting plans? Had she merely wanted a fresh start in New York? A new and exciting life with Gilbert, where nobody had known them?

A quick search of the Ellis Island records would confirm whether Annie had arrived in New York the summer of 1943. Eight months before Gilbert Moffat had supposedly died in the war.

I placed a gentle hand on Julia's. "I'm sorry. That's so sad you fell out of touch. Did you stay in touch with any of her family in the area?"

She shook her head.

Too bad. If there were family members around who'd known the truth, they might be more willing to divulge secrets decades later. There was a slight chance anyone was still alive. If Annie had lied to her friend, had she also lied to her family? Had they figured it out when she'd never showed up at her aunt's in New York? Or had they known the truth about her and the married man and insisted she at least save the family the humiliation and fabricate a tale?

"After Annie left for the States, her parents went to live with their married daughter in Australia." Julia gazed out the window. "Don't recall her name. Not sure what ever happened to her two brothers..." She shook her head in frustration.

"I'm sorry. I don't mean to upset you."

"Not at all, luv." She smiled. "'Tis nice talking about Annie. Haven't for some time now. Just wish I could remember more."

"You remember the important things. Your wonderful friendship and how much she meant to you."

The woman nodded, smiling. "Indeed. Oh, we were involved in some shenanigans, the two of us."

Like Biddy and me.

Julia shared stories of her and Annie's adventures. Train trips to Dublin, sneaking a nip of whiskey from their fathers' stashes, and taking Annie's father's tractor for a joyride. Before I realized it, I'd been there forty minutes, twenty-five minutes longer than my limit. I promised to visit again when I popped by to see Bernie McBride about the books I'd dropped off.

I hated to think Annie would have chosen a snake like Gilbert over Julia. If she'd regretted it, she'd had no family to go home to and would have been an outcast if locals had learned the truth. However, Julia would surely have forgiven her friend.

I found Biddy having her short nails painted bright pink by the mysterious woman from yesterday. The petite woman had on a blue pleated dress and cream-colored ballet slippers with pink satin bows. Her white hair was once again up in a loose bun. She and Biddy wore matching bright-pink lipstick and pink circles of blush on their cheeks. Biddy introduced me to her makeup artist, Winnie Dwyer, whose granddaughter worked for a cosmetic company and received free samples.

A colorful painting of St. Brigid hung on the wall over the bed. Ireland's only female patron saint was regarded as the Celtic goddess of healing. Based on the Irish calendar, St. Brigid's Day, February 1, signaled the end of winter and a time of renewal. The other walls displayed vintage theater posters, including Rudolph Nureyev in *Swan Lake* and the musical *A Chorus Line*.

"Worked at a theater in Dublin for years." Winnie glanced up while her shaky hand continued brushing pink polish on Biddy's nails. "'Twas a lovely time. Pay wasn't much, but I was able to keep several posters and had a bit role in many performances."

"Bet you met loads of celebrities," Biddy said.

A reminiscent smile curled the woman's thin pink lips. "Some, of course, thought a bit much of themselves, while others were absolutely lovely."

"I bet you have some interesting stories," I said.

Winnie nodded. "We'll have tea sometime." Finishing Biddy's manicure, she admired her work. Biddy's polished hangnails and cuticles matched her nails.

Biddy blew on her nails. "Tell my friend Mags here your theory about the skeleton."

The woman's smile faded, and a mysterious glint sparkled in her pale-blue eyes. "When I was nearly twenty, we had a farmhand who also did maintenance and grounds work for the Dunphys. I once saw the older Dunphy lad and him arguing behind the grocer. The fight ended with the Dunphy fella handing him a load of quid. The next day our man didn't show for work. I thought my parents should notify the garda. My father said farmhands came and went as they pleased. That the fella had merely fancied a change of scenery. Hard keeping good workers at the time, it was."

"Do you recall his name?" I asked.

"Went by Kerry, but 'twasn't his name. He was a blow-in from County Kerry. He hadn't any ties to the area. Still, I thought it odd at the time. Thought maybe the Dunphy fella had been paying our man off to leave the area for some reason. Now with them finding that skeleton, it makes sense. Maybe the Dunphy lad wanted his money back and killed the man. It's surely him." She placed a hand on her silver necklace, a St. Brigid's cross—a square in the middle with an arm radiating out from each corner.

"Any idea what year that would have been?" I asked.

"I was recently wed." She smiled. "Henri was a lovely man. We married in the spring of 1948, so would have been not long after that. I doubt there's anyone still around who knew the man, but I'll check."

"Do you know if the Dunphys had other workers or boarders who'd lived on the estate?" Like in the 1911 census, there might have been non-family members residing there.

Winnie shook her head. "Sorry, luv. Don't recall."

However, she remembered several interesting stories from her theater days. Before we knew it, a half hour had passed. I gave the woman my number and asked her to call if she learned the guy's name. I promised to pop back by soon for a visit.

Biddy chewed on her lower lip, studying her nails as we headed down the hall. "A good thing I didn't go with red. It might have been too flashy, drawing attention to my manicure."

The hot pink wasn't exactly subtle.

"I can't be removing it. Don't want to be offending sweet little Winnie if I return with unpolished nails."

We peeked in the quiet TV room, where a group was doing tai chi. So much for chatting with people to learn more theories. On the way to the car, Biddy shared several farfetched ones she'd heard from residents watching *Father Ted*. Winnie's story sounded the most plausible, but a drifter farmhand nicknamed Kerry from County Kerry wasn't much to go on. Did it somehow connect to Johnny's theory about the dodgy salesman who'd disappeared, leaving behind his suitcase? Even if it didn't, it appeared the Dunphys had some shady business going on with shifty characters.

Thirteen

FIFTEEN MINUTES OUT OF KILCARRIGY, Garda Higgins phoned Biddy that her car was available for pickup at the station. We turned around and headed back to town. A garda vehicle and small sporty red car sat in the lot. No small gray car.

Biddy glanced up and down the street at parked cars. "Don't see it, do ya?"

I shook my head.

Before I could recommend that she remove the circles of blush from her cheeks, Biddy bolted inside the station. Garda Higgins sat at a wood desk surrounded by light-blue and gray walls. The white-bearded man's curious gaze narrowed on Biddy's makeup, then recognition flickered in his eyes. She was the woman who'd uncovered the skeleton. Not some crazed clown on the loose that I'd captured.

Biddy managed a pleasant smile. "Here to collect my car."

"It's in the lot." He snatched up a set of keys that didn't

have Biddy's key chain from the Canary Islands. "One of the forensic fellas just dropped it off."

"Have you been out to see it?" she asked.

He shook his head.

Having been at the investigation site, he was familiar with Biddy's car.

She thrust out her hand, and he dropped the keys into her palm. "Suppose it'll do as long as the taxes and insurance aren't too expensive."

I shot Biddy an incredulous look. That car was worth at least three times her vehicle.

The man's gaze narrowed. "What do you mean you suppose it'll do? It's not your car?"

She reluctantly shook her head.

"I can't be giving you a car that isn't yours." He held out his hand for the keys.

"But you can be *taking* a car that isn't yours?"

"Your car is being checked for evidence." The officer's ruddy complexion turned even redder.

"For as long as you've had it, you could have been checking it for a new engine and tires." She tightened her grasp on the keys, then snapped her hand against her chest. "I'll be giving them back if you be telling me where my car is. I have the right to check on it." She eyed the officer. "Or haven't you a clue where it's at?"

"I'll call the fella straightaway and get this figured out. Your car will be here today."

Biddy glared at his hand, holding her ground.

I gave her a sharp nudge with my elbow.

She dropped the keys into his hand. "If I don't have my car today, I'll be giving you an invoice for a rental."

"That's grand."

Biddy's eyes widened. "You mean I could have been reimbursed for a rental?"

He shook his head. "Didn't say I'd be *paying* the invoice."

Biddy's cheeks turned red. She spun and stalked out of the station.

Back in the car, I recommended Biddy clean off her makeup with a wipe from my glove compartment. I questioned her about her weekend plans with Collin.

"I won't be going off if we're still investigating poor Skelly."

"I'm wondering why you didn't mention it."

She shrugged. "He just suggested it a few days ago. With everything going on, I'd completely forgotten about it until he brought it up today." Biddy scratched at her neck, a nervous habit.

"Why are you lying?"

She snapped her hand away from her neck. "Because I haven't a clue why I didn't tell you. Going away together for a weekend just seems so serious. I didn't know what you'd think. I don't know what *I* think about it."

"I think it's a great idea."

"You do?"

"Absolutely. Two or three days together should give you a better idea on how you feel about each other and how you get along."

"What if we don't get on?"

"Then you'll know."

"But what if I don't want to know?"

I shrugged. "You need to know."

"Like *you* need to know about *Ian*?" Biddy looked

pleased with her counterattack. "And don't tell me that's different. If you don't let him in enough to know how you feel about a relationship, you'll never have one. Good or bad."

I stared at the roundabout ahead and the exit for Mullingar. "I emailed him about Skelly two days ago, and he hasn't responded."

That took a bit of wind out of Biddy's argument. "I'm sure there's a logical explanation."

"Like maybe he saw our viral Twitter post?"

"He'd be ringing if he saw that."

I sighed. "Library is open late today. Let's check in with Edmond and Rosie. I'm in desperate need of more articles with clues."

Like one about a brutal break-in at the grocery store that had sent one of the Dunphy men to a Dublin hospital. I brought my laptop in with us so I could check Ellis Island records for Annie Fallon. I didn't know where to begin researching a drifter farmhand from Kerry. It'd be great if Winnie came through with his name.

While I parked in the library's lot, Biddy checked social media. Over 38,000 likes and 823 shares. I popped two ibuprofen. Upon entering the history room, I inhaled the intoxicating scent of vintage books and newspapers—a small collection of which weren't on microfilm. If cemeteries were my spa, archives were my aromatherapy. I'd found my first obituary here at the age of ten. Patrick Hickey. I'd laughed at the name. My older sister, Emma, had recently told me about hickeys. After reading the man's obit, I'd sworn I'd never allow a boy to give me a hickey on the neck since it'd remind me of poor Patrick. The guy had slipped on cow manure and fallen on a slab of cement. He'd bitten his tongue so hard he'd ended up with gangrene and died.

I would forever associate a hickey with gangrene.

Edmond was seated at a microfilm viewer, with Rosie on one side, Gretta on the other. The couple gave us faint smiles, whereas Gretta's hawklike gaze remained glued to the screen.

"How's it going?" I asked cautiously, surprised to see Gretta.

"Ah, grand," Edmond said.

Rosie gave me a tight smile.

Gretta glanced over from behind her reading glasses. "My printer hasn't arrived, and my laptop is small. Decided I'd be much more productive viewing papers on microfilm. I received your message, so keeping an eye out for missing women."

"Perfect. I'm also going to have you check the summer of 1943." When Annie had mysteriously left behind her best friend and family to never return. "Anything you come across about an Annie Fallon or her family. And if you all can watch for an article on a break-in at the Dunphys' grocery store. Not sure when, but it was bad enough to put one of the men in a Dublin hospital for weeks or months."

Gretta gave me a sharp nod. "Will do." Her determined gaze swooped back over to the viewer, and she continued scanning the newspaper.

"We came across a tidbit for you," Edmond said.

Rosie proudly handed me a copy of a small article highlighted in pink. *Dunphy's Grocer Looking at Expanding to Galway.* "Thought it might be a clue."

I smiled. "You never know. Thanks."

"Also found a bit on the older Mrs. Dunphy organizing

volunteers for the garden club's sale at the local fair. Mentioned many of the members' names in the group." She smiled, placing a hand on Edmond's arm. "Ah, remember going to the fair, Edmond? What a lovely time."

Edmond smiled. "Indeed, it was."

The cute couple reminisced about the fair while I sat at a back corner table and booted my laptop. Biddy camped out next to me, catching up on social media posts.

A fifteen-minute search of the Ellis Island records confirmed Annie hadn't arrived in New York anytime in 1943 with or without Gilbert Moffat.

The plot thickened.

"Bingo!" Gretta blurted out, startling Rosie.

Edmond placed a calming hand on Rosie's shoulder, and the woman's glare softened. I felt bad that Gretta's competitiveness was sucking the fun out of Edmond and Rosie's research time together. I had to think of a way to prevent Gretta from returning to the library tomorrow. Case in point why I wouldn't want to grow my business and have to manage employees. Knowing what you didn't want was as important as knowing what you wanted.

The printer hummed to life, and Gretta sprang from her chair. She snatched up the sheet of paper and read it out loud. "We ask that everyone keep Gilbert Moffat in their prayers. The brave man has gone off to war. Not a man to partake in fanfare in light of the grave situation facing the world at this time, he went off without celebration." Gretta thrust the paper at me, smiling proudly.

"Ah, fair play to ya," Biddy told Gretta. "That's a brilliant find. Might even be what cracks the case."

Gretta's look turned suspicious.

First tea and biscuits at the pub and now Biddy was praising the woman for her superior sleuthing skills?

The deep crease between Gretta's brows relaxed, and she gave Biddy an appreciative smile. "Thanks a million."

Biddy wore a pleased expression.

"What's the paper's date?" I asked.

"June 1943."

The same time Annie Fallon had supposedly sailed for America, yet she hadn't. If it was a coincidence that both events happened at the same time, where *had* Annie gone the summer of 1943? Same place as Gilbert Moffat?

Biddy and I picked up takeaway lasagna from the convenience store and went to my house for a late dinner and to regroup.

"Can't believe Garda Higgins never rang about my car. So much for checking on it straightaway. How could the forensics team have lost a car?" Biddy stuffed a forkful of cheesy pasta into her mouth.

Yeah, something seemed fishy. Yet if I agreed with Biddy, we'd spend the next hour coming up with theories about her car's mysterious disappearance instead of ones about Skelly.

I nodded at the glass of Bordeaux in my hand. "This is the best wine ever."

Biddy took another drink of the red wine, savoring the taste of blackberry, vanilla, and a hint of licorice. She relaxed back against the couch.

"We should get organized," I said.

"You need one of those whiteboards like they have on the

detective shows," Biddy said. "Where we can hang suspects' snaps and articles. Add and erase ideas. It's hard to be keeping track of this all."

Dozens of names filled my head from creating the Dunphy and Moffat family trees. My head was ready to explode. I ran up to my office and removed everything from the bulletin board on the wall and brought it downstairs along with a blue marker and printer paper. I propped the board up on the fireplace mantel.

I jotted *No. 1* on a piece of paper and added *Dodgy Suitcase Salesman*. "Hopefully, Johnny's friend can corroborate his story and add a few details, like the date and if it was Ernest or Oscar who was nearly killed in the break-in. I'm intrigued that it occurred at the same time a visiting salesman vanished, leaving behind his suitcase."

Biddy nodded. "I once forgot a necklace at a bed-and-breakfast on Achill Island. Called the place when I got home, and they posted it the next day. Who leaves a suitcase of clothes and toiletries in a hotel and never picks it up? I mean, wouldn't a traveling salesman be needing a suitcase to travel?"

"If the break-in happened after old man Dunphy died in 1946, maybe one son walked into the store and found his brother badly beaten up and the dodgy salesman lying dead on the floor."

Biddy sprang to her feet and started pacing. "The place was wrecked from the brawl, so it was easiest to claim there was a break-in."

I nodded, scribbling down our ideas. "The brother sneaks the dead body out the back and dumps it in his car. He then hauls the body and his nearly dead brother home, where the family decides he needs medical attention. Yet if they took him to an area doctor or hospital, there'd be too many nosey locals questioning what happened."

"After taking his brother to the A and E in Dublin, the fella goes back home and buries the body under the shed. It had to have happened before Kiernan's granny married Ernest. She'd never have stood for a dead body being buried under her garden shed with her three young lads living there."

"I haven't ruled out the woman having killed and buried her husband."

Biddy nodded. "True."

"The company ledgers might provide insight into the salesman's identity. If Johnny's friend can narrow down the time period, I could check them. Yet the grocer likely did business with a lot of regulars. We need to figure out which Dunphy brother ended up in the Dublin hospital." I added this to my to-do list.

I penned *No. 2* on a piece of paper, then wrote *Farmhand Kerry* and hung it on the board. "A drifter farmhand disappears after Oscar gave him a load of money. Did he return to Kerry or end up under the shed? Was the wad of cash a blackmail payment or Oscar's spur-of-the-moment idea to shut the man up? Perhaps Oscar didn't like being blackmailed and later offed the guy."

"I don't see how we'll ever identify some random blow-in from County Kerry in 1948."

"Winnie never mentioned if the guy left his stuff behind or if it vanished with him. I wonder if she remembers. That could definitely make a difference." I added that to my list of questions. "Something shady had been going on either with the grocery store or Oscar, and possibly Ernest. If we can figure out what it was, maybe that would help identify the man."

"Or *men*. If two men went missing around the same time, that might mean there's another skeleton buried in the yard."

"Maybe Johnny's friend's family has the hotel records from the 1940s boxed up in the attic that would list the guy's name. If he was a regular, maybe his name would stand out. It sounds like his business with Oscar was likely done off the books. I can see if anything in the Dunphy's grocer's ledgers looks sketchy."

As if I'd know sketchy if I saw it. Not in a business ledger anyway.

"Maybe the pub was running a brothel rather than an inn. And Suitcase Salesman and the Dunphys were investors."

"We'll hope it was a legit hotel, or they certainly wouldn't have kept a business ledger."

I jotted *No. 3* and *Gilbert Moffat* on a sheet of paper. "The war hero who never went to war." I tacked the newspaper article about Gilbert going off to war to the board and wrote *1943, same summer Annie Fallon vanished*. I added the article with the adultery charges filed against Gilbert and the charges he filed against the man. "Would be awfully coincidental if he and Annie Fallon left town at the same time and neither ever returned."

"I still kind of fancy the British secret agent with the Irish Free State pence in his pocket," Biddy said. "Even if Skelly was a bit dodgy, I'd like to think he was a patriotic fella."

"I agree, but let's stick to three theories for now."

Biddy checked her phone. "Janey," she muttered. "Our snap is now up to nearly fifty thousand likes and thirteen hundred shares."

We polished off the bottle of Bordeaux, and Biddy headed home to work on social media damage control ideas for ourselves, not just Kiernan. It was only a matter of time before someone outed us on Twitter. Like one of my sisters.

Preparing for an all-nighter, I counteracted my sleepy wine-induced haze with two cups of tea. My goal was to prove or disprove my Gilbert Moffat theory by piecing together the rest of his family tree and starting on Annie Fallon's.

An arrival of a text dinged on my cell. Ian. I tapped a finger against my phone, unsure if I wanted to learn his reaction to my Skelly story. I took the plunge and read it. His cell company had mistakenly disconnected his service, and the issue was finally resolved. He sounded concerned and curious about me having uncovered a skeleton. He hoped I was doing okay.

My shoulders relaxed at his reasonable response.

Now what could I be neurotic about?

Around 2:00 a.m. I was staring blurry-eyed at my computer screen about to quit for the night when I found an obit for Annie Fallon's brother. He'd died in County Cavan in 1964. Out-of-town funeral guests had included a Mrs. Gilbert Moffat from Belfast.

I about collapsed with relief and exhaustion.

For once I wasn't annoyed by the sexist archaic tradition of referring to a woman by her husband's name. *Annie* Moffat would have been a more common name than Gilbert. The couple had either been illegally married or had merely claimed to be husband and wife. I could tell Kiernan that his grandfather had been a cheating jerk rather than fertilizer under his grandmother's garden shed. That should make up for me threatening him for the second time. He'd be so relieved he'd follow through on his agreement to film the show at the castle hotel.

However, did I need more evidence?

Neither Gilbert's nor Annie's death was listed in the civil records index. If they'd died in Belfast, there might have been a death notice in the newspaper. I didn't have time to search decades of papers not knowing a death date. A search of the cemetery databases turned up nothing.

The obituary mentioning Mrs. Gilbert Moffat, Julia's story about Annie, and the fact that the couple had left town the same summer was enough for me and likely enough for Kiernan. He'd be happy to eliminate his grandmother as a murder suspect, his grandfather as a victim. It'd be different if Gilbert's name had been Patrick Murphy or John Kelly. You could walk into any pub in Ireland and call out either name and at least one or two men would answer to it. Whereas if I went on an all-night pub crawl through Belfast or Dublin and encountered even *one* Gilbert Moffat, I'd go out and buy lotto tickets.

I felt confident I'd found Kiernan Moffat's grandfather.

Fourteen

AFTER A FEW RESTLESS hours of sleep, I rolled out of bed at 8:00 a.m. eager to share my discovery with Kiernan. First, I wanted to discuss Gretta with Edmond and Rosie since I hadn't thought of a way to prevent Gretta from joining them at the library. I was meeting them at Edmond's for a quick chat, hoping a bit of insight into Gretta's fragile emotional state might make them more tolerant of the woman.

Edmond's home was much tidier and cozier with Rosie around. The man had been sweet on Grandma and taken her death as hard as I had. Thankfully, he and Rosie had started seeing each other last spring when they'd helped me solve the mystery of the Neils' stolen manuscript.

The stacks of genealogy and history books in Edmond's living room were a bit more organized. He removed a pile of books from a chair for me to sit across from them on the worn blue couch. Flames danced in a black cast-iron stove, the rustic scent of peat in the air.

I took a sip of tea, staring at a framed vintage photo of a nearby village hanging on the freshly painted light-gray walls.

I nibbled on a ginger biscuit, unsure how to approach the topic of Gretta.

"Are we being fired?" Rosie blurted out. "We're too slow compared to Gretta, aren't we?" She frowned, fidgeting with her pearl necklace.

"No, absolutely not."

"We can work faster," she said.

"Now, luv." Edmond placed a comforting hand on Rosie's knee. "Can't be working faster, or we might be missing something. Gretta may well be missing clues herself."

"This has nothing to do with your research," I said. "You've both found some great clues. I'd be lost without your help."

Rosie's features relaxed. "Well, you seem a bit nervous, so was afraid it was bad news."

"Not at all. But it has to do with Gretta."

The woman's fingers curled tightly around her pearl necklace.

"Gretta's having a difficult time right now. I think the story about her printer not working is an excuse to be around people." And not thinking about her upcoming DNA test and how it might change several people's lives.

Rosie sighed. "I need to be a more patient person. Even though the woman isn't easy at times and is fiercely competitive, that's no excuse for my behavior."

As if Rosie could be a better person.

"I'm not saying you're mean to Gretta, not at all. I just know she can be difficult, and I wanted you to realize she's going through a hard time."

Rosie nodded. "I need to let bygones be bygones."

What bygones?

Rosie didn't appear to want to discuss the matter, so I let it go, at least for now.

On the way to Kiernan's, I filled Biddy in on my discovery about Gilbert Moffat having run off to Belfast with Annie Fallon, never to return to Kilcarrigy.

I decided the element of surprise would work better than giving Kiernan a heads-up I would be paying him a visit. After the devastating news I'd delivered the other day about his grandpa Gilbert, he was likely back in a velvet robe and slippers, once again a viral video waiting to happen. Lucky for him, Biddy and I had shown up the last time and gone viral instead. Talk about taking one for the team. The guy owed me a favor, and I was about to call it in.

When ringing the doorbell repeatedly and pounding on the door didn't work, Biddy and I each tossed a small pebble up at the library window. It took me a half dozen tries before a pebble hit the glass. The appraiser appeared at the window, glaring down at us. He snapped the red drapes shut.

Biddy stalked to my car and laid on the horn.

The drapes opened, followed by the window.

"What do you want?" he shouted at me. "To tell me my dear granny was a black widow and Ernest is buried under the house?"

"I'm here to tell you it's more like a point five percent chance rather than a fifty percent chance Skelly is your grandfather Gilbert."

He slammed the window shut and disappeared.

Biddy and I waited impatiently until approaching footsteps finally sounded. The door flew open. The man had on the same tan slacks and blue oxford as the last time I'd seen him, along with the muddy velvet slippers. The previously crisply pressed clothes were now wrinkled, the shirt untucked from the pants. He nodded at the papers in my hand.

"Your grandpa Gilbert abandoned his wife and children and ran off with a young woman to Belfast."

Kiernan collapsed against the doorframe, letting out a rush of air. "Thank God." He stepped aside, allowing us to enter. Dried mud remained on the fancy Turkish rug and stairsteps.

Once upstairs in the library, I handed Kiernan the obituary noting Mrs. Gilbert Moffat had attended Annie Fallon's brother's funeral. I told him how Annie's friend Julia's story had helped me piece it together. Along with the newspaper bit asking the community to wish the brave man a safe return home from war. I'd decided not to bring a copy of the adultery charge filed against Gilbert. Let Kiernan believe Annie had been the guy's only unforgiveable indiscretion.

Kiernan shook his head. "Can't believe my grandmother fabricated such a story, making the man out to be a hero. Had to have been for the benefit of her children. The woman was a saint."

I nodded. She certainly had been. Who knew how many more adultery cases might pop up against Gilbert Moffat by the time my research assistants finished reviewing the papers.

"I'd already planned to return to work before that eejit gets the show canceled because viewers can't trust a word that comes out of the idiot's mouth. I was about to shower and get ready to head into Dublin. Have an interview scheduled so the media will stop hounding me."

"As your damage control manager, I should go with," Biddy said.

"Absolutely not. I can certainly handle an interview." He gave Biddy's nails a disapproving glance.

"But can you handle it *well*?" she said.

"How *well* have you been handling this supposed role of yours?" He scoffed.

"I have social media under control."

More like out of control, but at least the focus was on us rather than Kiernan.

"I'm not wasting my time commenting on negative posts and getting into heated arguments—I'm creating new ones to generate positive publicity with some brilliant hashtags. Have paid to promote a few of the more popular ones. Women are all over the snap of you in the black suit and cobalt-blue paisley tie at that Dublin fundraiser last year. That tie brought out the blue in your eyes. The one of you at the antique book fair in London last summer is seeing loads of comments from your peers. And I found a photo of that English landlord who owned the estate prior to the Dunphys in nineteen hundred. The wretched-looking man has murderer written all over him. Seeing as the 1928 coin hasn't been disclosed, I thought it was a great idea to direct suspicions at him."

Blown away, Kiernan and I both stared at Biddy in shocked awe. This was the first I'd heard any of this. I'd figured she'd been spending her time monitoring our photo's stats on Twitter.

"Right, then. Bravo." Kiernan smiled at Biddy. "You appear to have a firm grasp on the social media aspect. Thank you."

Biddy blinked in surprise at his appreciation.

"As far as I know, neither my siblings nor coworkers have come to my rescue on social media. Haven't heard a word from either brother and only from the producer to demand I not come into work." He turned to me. "And thanks a million for clearing my grandmother's name should her story somehow become public knowledge."

"Does this mean the filming is back on at Dalwade Castle?" Biddy asked.

He nodded. "A deal is a deal."

Since when? However, the man's sincere gratitude and softened exterior, bordering on humble, increased my trust in him. Not completely, yet excitement zipped through me.

"I'm researching several other theories I'd like to confirm before I share with you," I said. "Did you ever hear mention of Ernest's older brother, Oscar?"

He pondered that a moment, then nodded. "Didn't recall his name, but the man ran a shop in Dublin, I believe."

"Galway maybe?" According to the article Rosie had found.

"No, it was Dublin."

"Do you recall him ever being involved in some dubious dealings?"

His eyes widened. "What sort of dubious dealings?"

Like burying a body under the shed.

"I have no clue. From the stories I've heard, it sounds like he was a shady character."

"Well, he might have been, but Ernest certainly wasn't."

"Ever hear about Ernest or Oscar being involved in a break-in that nearly killed one of them and landed him in a Dublin hospital?"

"Would guess that was Oscar. I'd surely have heard about Ernest being beaten nearly to death."

Just like Kiernan's family folklore told the story about a body being buried under his grandmother's garden shed?

While we were searching for a local place to eat until the nursing home's lunch hour had ended, Ita phoned that Johnny and his buddy from Kilcarrigy were at the pub. We drove straight there while they were hopefully still on their first pint.

Not that I thought I'd get much more information out of his friend. I wanted to make sure I got the *same* information out of the guy as I had Johnny. Besides Johnny possibly having embellished the story over a pint, he might have forgotten exactly how the story went and taken creative liberty to fill in the holes. I'd heard some tall tales in McCarthy's over the years. Sadly, the one about a sheep chasing me into the pub, where I'd done a record leap onto the bar, was true.

A few locals sat at tables, eating sandwiches or the pub's famous pizza. Ita threw in a pepperoni pizza for us. Unlike Johnny's short and stocky stature, his friend Andy was tall and lean, wearing a Van Morrison T-shirt. The two men pulled their chairs out from the bar, and Biddy and I slipped onto two stools across from them. Andy's story matched Johnny's. He confirmed it was Oscar who'd taken a brutal beating during the store's break-in.

It appeared Oscar was the dodgy Dunphy.

"Was in a Dublin hospital for some time," Andy said.

"Was sweet on a nurse and ended up marrying her. Opened a grocery store over there."

"Do you know about when the break-in occurred?" I asked.

"Summer of 1948. Just after I was born. My mum said the whole fiasco was nearly the death of her when she had two wee ones at home to be minding."

Winnie had mentioned that Farmhand Kerry had vanished in spring of 1948. Maybe she considered June spring, whereas Andy considered it summer. Regardless, it was around the same time.

"Did Oscar come around much after he moved?" I asked.

The guy shrugged. "I never saw the fella. From what I heard, his leaving the family business caused a bit of a feud between the brothers."

It made sense that if Oscar had killed Suitcase Salesman, he'd have left town and never returned.

"Do you think there's a chance your family's hotel ledgers are around from that time?"

Andy chuckled. "Don't think my mum kept ledgers for the inn. Was more of a cash basis. Pub patrons wouldn't have wanted it known how often they'd had to crash at the inn. My cousin runs the place now. Might still have 'em from the pub somewhere in the back."

Biddy and I let out disappointed sighs.

"Do you know if your mum filed a report with the guards about the fella disappearing without his suitcase?" Biddy asked.

He shook his head. "She didn't. That was the oddest bit of all. When the fella never returned for his suitcase, my mum called in on the Dunphys with it, wondering if they'd be seeing him soon or had his contact information. He hadn't left a phone number with the hotel. Mrs. Dunphy said she was too upset to be dealing with such a thing when her son was in a Dublin hospital. My mum said she'd be taking the suitcase to the garda and let them sort it out. When she pulled into the garda station, Ernest Dunphy was right behind her. He apologized his mum hadn't been thinking clearly, and of course, they'd be getting the suitcase back to the fella. My mum never saw the fella again. Makes ya wonder if the family hadn't wanted the guards involved."

Biddy and I exchanged intrigued glances.

"Sounds a bit suspicious if you ask me," Biddy said.

"My mum let it go, having enough going on with two wee ones at home."

I bought the men another pint. Now I knew it was Oscar who'd gone off to Dublin in 1948 around the same time Farmhand Kerry and Suitcase Salesman had both vanished. I was even more convinced that Skelly was the salesman.

Maybe Bernie McBride had found more info on the grocery store in his history books, including Oscar Dunphy's shop in Dublin. I could also check Dublin city directories for that time and for Oscar and the nurse's marriage record.

I called Gretta to search the 1948 papers for the break-in. Hopefully, Edmond and Rosie weren't offended that I appeared to be relying more heavily on Gretta's research. They shouldn't take offense when that was just the way it was working out. Everything we were uncovering pointed to the same time period.

The summer of 1948.

Fifteen

ON THE WAY to the nursing home, Biddy worked on social media posts and checked for Kiernan's interview on a Dublin newspaper's page.

"Janey," Biddy shrieked. "Our photo has seventy-two thousand likes and twenty-seven hundred shares. It's gaining momentum."

Like a runaway train about to derail. My stomach clenched.

As soon as the appraiser's interview posted, I pulled onto a side road to watch. The interview began with him stating the deceased deserved an identity and a proper burial. That if the garda didn't ensure he got it, Kiernan would.

"Nearly quoting ya word for word," Biddy said. "At least he's coming across heroic. Women will be going mad for him. The interview might go viral."

However, the interview quickly went downhill when the reporter questioned if Kiernan planned to be as forthcoming about Skelly when the murderer turned out to be a Moffat.

Kiernan defended his family, guaranteeing a member hadn't put a hole in the victim's skull.

Biddy gasped. "Have the guards released that it was a murder and Skelly's missing a chunk of skull?"

I shook my head, breaking out in a sweat. "He walked right into that one. Nasty woman. Speaking of nasty women..." I pointed out a blond woman lurking in the background. "That's the producer. What's she doing just standing there? Trying to get the man fired?"

"You know she is. Stop the train wreck!" Biddy yelled at the woman.

"Somebody do something!"

Thankfully, our screaming drowned out the rest of the interview, which quickly ended when Kiernan bolted. Biddy and I collapsed against our seats, emotionally drained.

Biddy cleared her hoarse throat. "Hashtag *skeletonscandal* must be going mad right now. We'd have to be posting nude snaps of ourselves rolling around in the estate's mud to divert attention from that disaster. Bet he's regretting I'm not there doing damage control. Not sure if I am."

Once recovered, we cruised past the garda station. No small gray car sat in the lot. Biddy currently wasn't mentally up to dealing with the additional stress, so we continued to the nursing home in silence. We stopped off at Julia's room, where she was sleeping in her comfy rose-colored chair with a content look on her face. The coconut-scented room reminded me of suntan lotion and weekend trips with the McCarthys to a beach in Wexford. We'd frozen our butts off swimming in the Irish Sea.

I'd decided not to tell Julia that Annie had run off with Gilbert Moffat. Knowing her best friend had remained nearby in Northern Ireland, without having contacted her in seventy years, would break the woman's heart. It'd break mine if Biddy did that to me.

In Winnie's room, the woman was kneeling on a blue rug at the foot of her bed, eyes closed, hands together, praying to St. Brigid's painting.

"We should leave," I whispered.

Winnie's eyes opened, and she peered over at us.

"So sorry," Biddy said. "Didn't mean to be disturbing ya."

"Not a' tall, luv." She grasped ahold of the footboard and pulled herself to her feet, covered with pink ballet slippers. "Sorry I haven't rung. Haven't spoken with anyone who remembers our fella. Sadly, few still around from that time and the fella wasn't 'round here for long." She smiled at Biddy's manicure, which remained intact.

"No worries," I said. "Do you recall if he left behind his belongings or not?"

Her gaze narrowed. "I'm thinking he must have left 'em or his leaving wouldn't have seemed as odd as it had. He'd surely have had no more than a change or two of clothes and a few pairs of wool socks."

"Do you remember anything else about the Dunphys?" I asked. "Like the break-in at their store?"

Winnie brushed a purple fingernail over her pink glossed lips. "Now that you mention it, the break-in happened shortly after our man left town. A few weeks or months maybe. Hadn't thought of the two being related at the time, since the fella was gone. Do you think they were? That our fella returned to town and broke into the store?"

I shrugged, not wanting to lead a witness. However, I

hadn't mentioned the robbery occurred in 1948 same as Farmhand Kerry's disappearance. Yet the guy had disappeared prior to the break-in.

"I recall the one Dunphy lad had to manage the shop when his brother was hospitalized. Didn't hand out nearly as many free sweets to the children as the other lad. He was a nice enough fella, as was his wife. Don't recall her name, but her first husband was killed in the war."

I wasn't about to correct her on that one.

Nice to have the break-in confirmed from someone besides Johnny's friend. Winnie promised to call should she remember the farmhand's name or anything else about him.

I paused on our way down the hallway to Bernie McBride's room. "Winnie's story has the farmhand leaving months before the break-in. I can't see the guy having returned when Oscar had given him a wad of cash to leave. Why chance it?"

"Maybe the Kerry fella had blown through it all buying rounds in the pub and came looking for more."

I shook my head. "I don't see how the guy was involved in Skelly's murder. Seems more of a coincidence."

Biddy nodded. "That salesman disappearing without his suitcase and then Ernest acting suspicious, chasing down that inn owner before she could drop it at the garda station, seems much more mysterious to me."

Bernie McBride was seated at a small table filled with stacks of history books, paging through one.

"Ah, *two* lovely lasses. My lucky day."

Biddy introduced herself.

"Thanks a million for the books, luv," he told me.

"Haven't had a chance to read 'em. Still searching for information that might help you with the Dunphys." He snapped his fingers. "Speaking of my lucky day reminds me of that Oscar fella. He used to flick a penny off the top of his thumb, straight up into the air. No matter how high, he always caught it. If one of us lads guessed heads or tails correctly, he got a free sweet in the shop. Us kids always won of course. He'd say, 'Now it's *your* lucky penny.'"

Biddy and I exchanged shocked glances.

Was Skelly...Oscar Dunphy?

Or was it merely a coincidence that Skelly had a lone 1928 pence on him?

"The coin once slipped out a hole in the fella's pants pocket when he was delivering us groceries. I found it on the ground where his car was parked and returned it to him. He gave me a *ten* pence for having returned a pence. Must have been an important penny. He assured me my honesty would bring me good luck. A week later, a large oak fell over, missing my bedroom roof by mere centimeters. Fella was spot-on about the lucky penny."

"Sounds like he was a nice guy," Biddy said.

"To us kids anyway. Had more than his share of rows with adults in the area."

"Yeah, we came across an article about a dispute with a supplier, over Oscar not giving him a fair price on rashers and pork."

Bernie shrugged. "Not certain 'bout that. He left the area when I was a young lad. His brother minded the shop after that. A nice fella but a bit stingy with the free sweets. Although he'd give me a five pence for making a delivery or doing odd jobs now and then." He frowned at his stacks of books. "Sorry for not having found more information or being of much help. Will keep searching."

"You're grand," Biddy said. "A lovely story about the lucky penny."

That might have just helped crack the case.

I'd expected the man to have found a historical photo or article in one of his books, which would provide a clue to solving the mystery. Who knew it'd be a lucky penny story from his childhood?

"How can Skelly *not* be Oscar?" Biddy said as we headed out the front door toward my car.

"Perhaps the penny dropped out a hole in his pocket when he was burying the body. Oscar was the victim or the murderer and Suitcase Salesman was the other...unless Ernest was the killer. I wonder if the estate transferred to Ernest in 1948, the same year he took over the family business. I'll have to check the land records. Oscar leaving the area would have been quite a windfall for him."

Biddy nodded. "Ernest is looking more and more guilty."

"If Oscar was the *victim*, Ernest had to have been involved somehow, or he'd have known if Oscar never returned from his hospital stay in Dublin. The family would have filed a missing person's report if they weren't involved or at least aware of Oscar's murder. And who besides family would have fabricated the story of Oscar marrying a nurse and opening a shop in Dublin if it's not true? And if Oscar was the *killer*, he'd have moved to Dublin not wanting to answer questions on the missing salesman or raise suspicions."

"This is bad." Biddy shook her head. "Fierce bad."

"I just delivered good news to Kiernan. I don't want to be the bearer of bad news again. He'll take Ernest having been a murderer way worse than my theory that his grandpa was buried under the shed. Well, maybe not worse, since that would have made his grandma a killer. His grandma not having offed his grandpa had lessened the blow of the fake medal and bogus war-hero story. How am I going to lessen the blow that Ernest, the man's real-life hero, might have been a killer? The man inspired the appraiser's love for books and was the reason he'd chosen his career. He'd influenced Kiernan's future, his destiny."

"He'd also been a hero, saving Kiernan's grandmother and his father from a life of destitution. Thanks to Ernest, Kiernan's father received a good education and raised the family in a prominent Dublin suburb."

For Kiernan's sake, I was remaining optimistic that Oscar was the killer, not the victim. I needed proof that Oscar had married a nurse in Dublin and opened a grocery shop.

I pulled up in front of the pub, dropping Biddy off to have dinner with Collin, who was outside chatting on his phone.

"Case is almost solved," I said as she stepped from the car. "You and Collin can go off to Wicklow next weekend."

Biddy nodded faintly. "Unless another case comes up."

"You're going."

She slammed the door and walked toward the pub. The couple kissed hello, then Biddy headed inside and Collin headed toward my car. I rolled down the window.

He smiled. "Hey, Mags. What's the craic?"

"One step closer to solving the mystery."

"Ah, that's grand."

I nodded. "You guys can go away for the weekend."

His smiled faded, and he shot a nervous glance toward the pub. "A bit odd Biddy hadn't told you about our plans, isn't it? I mean, she tells you everything."

"Not *everything*. Honestly, it's been so crazy with the filming and the skeleton case, we haven't talked about much else."

He frowned, not looking reassured. "I'm thinking maybe she doesn't fancy a weekend away with me."

"She totally does," I lied. "Just has a lot on her mind right now."

Was Collin rethinking their getaway? Maybe Ita's engagement comment had freaked him out as well.

Biddy poked her head out of the pub and peered curiously at us. "Pizza's nearly done."

"I best be going," Collin said. "See ya, Mags."

Biddy would be calling the second he left, drilling me about our conversation.

I went home and removed Gilbert Moffat's information from the bulletin board. A tremendous sense of relief washed over me, no longer having Kiernan's grandfather on the possible victims list. Yet I hadn't a clue how to identify Farmhand Kerry and Suitcase Salesman. So I searched for evidence that Oscar had lived in Dublin in 1948 and later years. First I confirmed that the land records showed the estate's home had transferred from Oscar to Ernest in 1948. Interesting.

No death record or grave was online for Oscar. No Dunphy's grocer listed in the 1948-1950 Dublin city directories. No marriage record for Oscar and a nurse in Dublin or

Ireland. However, if Oscar was the killer, maybe he'd fled the country and hidden out on a South Pacific island. Mortified that Oscar had killed a man, the family had fabricated a story about his marriage to a lovely nurse in Dublin. Similar to Isobel's war-hero tale.

I stared at the stack of documents and a ledger from Kiernan. Why had only one business ledger been in the safe? Why hadn't the others been with it? I slipped the green cloth-covered book from the pile and opened it. Although I despised accounting and had little business knowledge, it only took me fifteen minutes to realize the ledger wasn't for the grocery store. Well, in a roundabout way it was.

It appeared Oscar had been a loan shark. He'd been loaning locals money at an insanely high interest rate. When a supplier couldn't make payments, he subtracted the amount from what the store owed him for goods. Like the Sheehan man, who'd filed charges against Oscar for not paying him the agreed-upon amount for his rashers and pork. I checked the ledger's 1933 entries and found Sheehan's name crossed off and a new supplier written in. Had the guy known Oscar was going with another supplier and had nothing to lose, so he'd filed charges, desperate for money? Previously, no man had likely dared to turn Oscar in for fear he'd tell the man's wife that he'd borrowed money for paying off gambling debts or a tab at the pub. Maybe Farmhand Kerry had been a collector. Oscar had needed some way to get money from those who weren't doing business with the grocer. He couldn't take it out of their pay.

Had Ernest found out about his brother's illicit dealings and that he was swindling their neighbors, so he'd whacked him? Had inheriting the estate and store been a bonus for Ernest rather than his motive?

The doorbell rang.

I was surprised to see Edmond, Rosie, and Gretta standing as a united team. They whisked inside, talking excitedly.

I held up a hand. "What did you find?"

Rosie graciously nodded at Gretta to share the news.

"We found an article on the break-in at the grocery store in 1948." Gretta must have found it since she was searching that year. Nice of her to give them credit as a team. "Following the break-in, Ernest returned to town to run the family business. It appears he'd been gone a few years."

"His dad died in 1946, and Oscar had inherited the house and several acres," I said. "He might have kicked Ernest out or Ernest was upset and left." Maybe Ernest had known about the loan shark operation, so Oscar's inheritance had added salt to the wound. "I wonder if Ernest had also quit the family business because of his father's will."

"Ernest's return was like a hero's homecoming celebration," Rosie said.

Edmond nodded. "Like one of those New York City ticker-tape parades I've seen on the tellie. Where Ernest would have been sitting on the back of a convertible and driven through the streets while the entire city tossed confetti from the upper windows of their flats or offices."

Gretta smiled earnestly. "The article had several quotes by locals who were over the moon to have Ernest return to run the family business. Not one word of sympathy for Oscar, who was supposedly on his deathbed in Dublin."

The entire town might have known Ernest had killed

Oscar and that was the reason for celebration. Nobody would have turned the hero in to the garda. Strange how the children from that time had fond memories of Oscar and his lucky penny and free sweets. Perhaps the man giving kids free candy was a way of earning their trust at a young age so he could later swindle them out of their money as adults.

"This calls for a celebratory drink at my house," Edmond said.

I smiled. "Thanks, but I have some research to do."

Rosie turned to Gretta. "Would you like to join us?"

A twinkle of surprise glistened in Gretta's gray eyes. She gave Rosie a grateful smile. "Thanks a million for the invite. But Tommy has been on his own for dinner the past few nights. I plan to make him a roast. Will definitely be celebrating with a glass of wine though."

"Ah, that's grand." Rosie smiled. "Another time, then."

"Indeed, another time," Edmond said.

My three excited assistants left, off for their celebratory drinks. I didn't feel like celebrating. The thought of Ernest, Kiernan's hero, having been the killer made my stomach toss. I hadn't shared my theory with Edmond, Rosie, and Gretta. I hadn't even wanted to share it with Kiernan, who called minutes after they'd left and asked me to come over. I hadn't planned to see him until I had more info. I didn't want him to cancel the Dalwade filming again unless I was confident Ernest was the killer.

At the moment, I was leaning toward confident.

Oscar's signature penny was a great clue, but it might take DNA evidence to solve the mystery, if a living Dunphy relation could be located.

Ernest hadn't had children with Isobel or any other

woman that I'd found. If Oscar had kids, they might still live on a South Pacific island. Ernest's younger unmarried sister had been buried with his parents. I hadn't come across the older sister, whose married name was included in the will. If any of the siblings had children and grandchildren, why hadn't one of them contacted Kiernan or the guards? The story had made the news in Scotland. Maybe uncovering buried skeletons in a yard wasn't uncommon in many places, so it wasn't newsworthy worldwide.

I had to handle this next visit with Kiernan more professionally and compassionately than I had the last one. Telling him the man he'd admired was possibly a killer would be way worse than a cheating grandpa he'd never known. I'd keep that to myself for now, not having confirmed the killer part. The only thing I knew was *Oscar* was likely the killer or victim. Now knowing Kiernan wasn't a heartless dodgy scam artist, at least not as heartless as I'd once thought, would make it difficult.

The appraiser having a compassionate and sentimental side was almost a stranger thing to uncover than a buried skeleton under the man's tree.

After the train-wreck interview, I assumed Kiernan was once again hiding out at the estate, avoiding social media and the internet. He wasn't answering his phone, so I headed over to Kilcarrigy.

Kiernan greeted me at the door in his dried muddy velvet slippers and green robe over blue satin pajamas. He appeared beaten down from his interview. Gone was his usual arrogant and self-confident attitude. He shuffled up the stairs to the library, where dramatic orchestra music played like from a movie in which an entire country had just been taken out by a meteor.

Kiernan dropped onto the couch. "Have some good news." Not even the faintest smile curled his lips. "The garda won't be pursuing an investigation. The bones have likely been in the ground less than seventy years but more than fifty. There are no known relatives demanding justice or needing closure, and the killer is likely dead."

"That's what you wanted, isn't it?"

He nodded faintly. "Suppose you saw my interview?"

I nodded reluctantly.

"Not one of my finer moments."

His absolute worst moment I'd ever witnessed.

"To think I once granted that wretched reporter an exclusive interview. And that's the thanks I get." He grabbed a bottle of sparkling water off the cocktail table, too depressed for whiskey, or perhaps he was out.

"Once it's announced there won't be an investigation, she'll be sinking her teeth into someone else's business, guaranteed. And people will be tweeting about some celebrity's affair or botched Botox."

"People turn on a dime. Not a faithful fan in the lot of 'em," Kiernan said.

"That's not true. Biddy mentioned all the support you've had from fans and peers."

"It's not merely brutal fans letting me down, but coworkers and family. A coworker nicking my grandfather's medal is one thing, but not one of them has come to my rescue during this entire circus. I apparently have no friends.

You and Biddy are the only ones who've had my back. Seeing as the authorities aren't pursuing an investigation and you have no conclusive evidence as to the victim's identity, you can stop researching. I'll stand by my agreement to shoot an episode at that castle."

My excitement about *Rags to Riches Roadshow* exposure for the castle hotel was dampened by the fact that I *did* have clues about Skelly's identity.

Noticing my hesitation, Kiernan quirked a curious brow. "You *don't* have hard evidence for any of your theories, do you?"

I twisted my mouth in contemplation.

He collapsed back against the couch. "Bloody lovely."

I dropped my shoulders in defeat and shared Bernie McBride's story about Oscar's lucky penny. The man's loan shark business. That the entire town had likely wanted the guy dead.

"I believe the coin slipped from Oscar's pocket when he was burying the salesman, who'd likely discovered the ledger," I assured him. "Then Oscar fled the country after murdering the man. His family was mortified and came up with that Dublin story to protect their reputation and rebuild the family business's reputation."

"What if Oscar was the victim? How couldn't Ernest have known his brother went missing? Or had he known because he was the bloody killer? It's one thing if a killer managed to bury a body on the grounds without the family's knowledge, but how could Oscar not have been the victim with the penny?" Kiernan rubbed his forehead. "That's it. I quit. I'm done spending my life in the spotlight, having my every move critiqued, even when they aren't true. The press would have a field day with this one."

I shook my head vigorously. "I'm not saying Ernest was the killer."

"You aren't saying he wasn't either. And the media has proven they care little about the truth as long as it makes headlines or goes viral."

Tell me about it.

Skelly deserved a name and identity. However, I couldn't allow a dead man to ruin Kiernan's *life*.

"I'm not pursuing the victim's identity," I said.

Surprise flickered in the man's blue eyes, then dimmed. "I'm still quitting. Sorry if your castle goes to ruins, but my life is in ruins."

"I'm not quitting so you'll agree to remain on the show and film at Dalwade Castle. I'm seriously worried about this destroying your life. You're one of the most knowledgeable antique book experts ever. You should continue doing what you love." Except for his involvement in any dodgy dealings. I wanted to believe there were less of those than I'd once imagined.

"I'm going to sell the estate and travel," he mused. "Get away from the dreary weather. Find a villa in southern Italy..."

This house had likely meant as much if not more to the appraiser than the career it had influenced. It would be like me selling my house and Grandma's legacy. Like I'd nearly done a year ago. A week ago I'd never have dreamed anything was more important to the man than fame, fortune, and his watch collection.

He wasn't the only one feeling defeated, disheartened,

and doomed. A good thing I hadn't given my family false hope. The show would no longer provide potential hotel guests worldwide with a peek inside the medieval castle. With the cost of repairs and refurbishments, we couldn't afford to buy exposure like that.

Yet we couldn't afford not to.

Sixteen

MY PHONE RANG on the nightstand, jarring me awake at 7:00 a.m. Unknown caller. I rolled over and buried my head in the pillow.

Depressed about my conversation with Kiernan, I'd gone to bed just three hours ago. What a loss for everyone. Kiernan was quitting his dream job, likely to be replaced by a coworker who wasn't qualified to work a newsstand. The castle's filming was off. If we didn't come up with a creative and economical marketing plan, the place might not survive. Skelly would remain unidentified and buried in an unmarked plot at some random cemetery rather than with his family.

My phone dinged the arrival of a voicemail.

I rolled out of bed and slipped the phone into the pocket of my flannel jammies. I trudged down the spiral staircase in Berber slippers to the kitchen. I made a double-bagged cup of tea and sat at the table, peering out the window at the sheep grazing on a ridge in the distance. I listened to the voicemail.

Winnie Dwyer had remembered something that might prove important and asked that I call her ASAP. Farmhand

Kerry's actual name was not of high importance when I was no longer pursuing the investigation and justice for Skelly...was it? I'd let down Skelly and violated my professional ethics.

However, I'd done the right thing.

Hadn't I?

Kiernan would have to live with the nagging curiosity as to whether his hero had been a killer.

Could *I* live with it?

I couldn't live without money. I signed into my work email to sort through the new ones for potential clients. Over three hundred new emails brought a smile to my face until I opened the first one. A British archaeologist wondered how we'd come across the skeletal remains and our excavation process. Another was from the nasty reporter who'd ambushed Kiernan in the interview, wanting to question me about having uncovered the skeleton. Reporters, archaeologists, museums, haunted tour guides, and hundreds of nosey people wanted the scoop on our involvement with Skelly! Near the top of the inbox was a second email from a potential client that I had moved to the Pending folder. In one sentence she informed me she no longer needed my services.

Had she seen our viral post, or was her timing merely a coincidence? Regardless, being known as a skeleton scavenger and body snatcher was not good for my genealogy business or my leadership role in the cemetery restoration project. What if Archie had no choice but to fire me because volunteers were worried that I'd be digging up Lord Kerr's skeleton!

Fingers flying across the keyboard, I was able to access Twitter without an account. I found Gaelic Gobshite's page.

His post with our photo now tagged Biddy and the *Rags to Riches Roadshow* page.

Who'd leaked our names to the jerk?

We'd feared someone might eventually identify us in the viral post, yet I was seething. Heart racing, I snatched my phone off the table and called Biddy.

"Serious, are ya?" Biddy shrieked. "Had someone recognized us from our snap on the *Rags to Riches Roadshow* page? We were in full costume, makeup, and our hair looked absolutely gorgeous. Not a thing like our horrible snap on Twitter."

"Right? It has to be someone who knows our involvement with the investigation and Kiernan. Outside of Edmond, Rosie, Gretta, and my dad, I haven't mentioned it to anyone. I mean, we've chatted with others about it but never flat out discussed our role. Can't imagine that the nursing home residents we've talked to about it would even be on social media."

"I'm messaging Gaelic Gobshite. Ring ya back."

Click.

While Biddy was in hot pursuit of the jerk who'd outed us to the world, I stared at the sheep in the distance, trying to lower my heart rate. What would I do if this damaged my genealogy career? Ancestry research was my passion. No way was I going back to working seasonal or temporary jobs. However, I would be going to Galway to hunt down the gobshite!

My phone rang. Biddy.

"The show's producer! I told that manky scumbag Gaelic Gobshite we're suing him for an invasion of privacy for publishing our names. He says the producer messaged him our names and authorized him posting them. I informed him she's not our bloody boss and to take our names off. Ya know he won't. Not one word speaking out in Kiernan's defense has been posted on the show's website or social media, so she outs *us*?"

Anger ripped through me like gale-force winds. I leaped to my feet. "Be ready in fifteen minutes. We're heading to Dublin, where the show's filming!"

A half hour later we zipped down the motorway toward Dublin, brainstorming horrible things to do to the producer. Way worse than the killer bees or ants in a guy's knickers scenarios. I filled Biddy in on my visit to Kiernan and promise not to pursue Skelly's identity.

"Mad, are ya? We can't drop this case even if the castle's no longer involved. What about poor Skelly?"

My phone rang on the console next to me.

Unknown caller. Winnie Dwyer.

I told Biddy about the woman's earlier voicemail message.

"What if she has more details than the farmhand fella's name?" Biddy said. "We need to go see her."

"I promised Kiernan I'd stop investigating."

"As if the man doesn't go back on his promises. Signed a contract and still went back on his promise to film at Dalwade."

True...

Right now I had to focus my energy on making sure the producer's plan to get Kiernan canned backfired. When we were done with her, the show would be looking for a new producer, not a new appraiser!

☘ ☘

Rags to Riches Roadshow was on location at the Irish Museum of Modern Art, west of Dublin's city center and just off a main highway. The modern artwork was housed in a restored seventeenth-century stone building that was once the Royal Hospital. The elegant facade and fancy gardens were a contrast to the interior's artwork depicting contemporary values and making bold statements. Our security guard buddy was at the door. A few flirty smiles gained us access to the film set.

We walked down a stark white hallway and encountered a thirtyish-year-old-guy dressed in an orange suit, yellow vest, and lime-green button-up shirt, his short hair gelled into a frenzy.

"Can you please tell me where the loo is?" Biddy asked.

He strode right past us and shot a rude response over his shoulder. "As if I work here."

Biddy sneered at the guy disappearing into a room. "What an eejit. He doesn't have to work here to know where the loo is. And that's precisely how I'd expect an employee or volunteer at a modern art museum to dress."

We located the loo, then found the producer in a white room with Picassoesque artwork on the walls. The lighting guy and cameraman were busy setting up across the room. We marched over to the woman.

"You should be ashamed," I told her. "If you can't maintain a professional working relationship after a personal one ends, then you shouldn't become involved with a coworker."

"That's none of your business." She squared her shoulders in her green pantsuit blazer.

I gave her the evil eye. "Yeah, it is. Kiernan is our friend. He's being brutally attacked by the mass media and even worse by social media. You and your coworkers have done nothing to stick up for him. Is your hurt pride worth losing the best appraiser this show has ever had?"

Her shoulders dropped. "What do you mean *lose* him?"

He hadn't called and quit last night?

"How long do you think he can put up with the bullying and lack of respect?" I said.

"We saw you lurking in the background during his train-wreck interview, yet ya did nothing," Biddy said. "Proud of yourself, are ya? The act of a scorned woman, not a top reality show's producer, unless it's retitled *Nags and Witches Roadshow*. How would your boss feel about that?"

"And how would he feel about the show being sued because its producer violated our privacy on Twitter?"

That made number three on our list of people to sue. As if we had money to sue *one* person.

Rather than ripping us to shreds, a look of regret and embarrassment washed over the woman's face.

The funky guy in the orange suit walked up. "What's going on here?"

"Still looking for the loo," Biddy quipped. "If you don't know where it is, then off with ya."

"Yeah, this is none of your business," I said.

"Most certainly is." He jutted out his chin in defiance. "I'm the rare and vintage book appraiser."

Kiernan's archenemy.

Biddy's gaze narrowed on the appraiser-wannabe's hideous outfit. "Who dresses you, the Joker? You should be working at a comic book shop. This is set of an antique show, not *Batman*. And everyone knows Boris Pasternak wrote *Dr. Zhivago*, not Leo Tolstoy."

Bravo, Biddy! I couldn't have remembered the author's name.

She turned to the producer. "Are you responsible for this idiot filling in for Kiernan Moffat? What is he, your boyfriend?"

"I'm her cousin," the guy snapped.

The woman's worried gaze darted around to make sure her coworkers hadn't overheard she'd hired a rellie instead of an expert appraiser. They'd surely figured out the unqualified part.

"Everyone needs to stop being bitter and petty and start being supportive," I demanded.

"Whoever manages the show's social media should be sacked for not working this craziness to the show's advantage. There are more positive social media posts than negative ones. The nasty ones just attract more trolls. Not only are there thousands of adoring fans who'd stop watching the show, but also peers who respect the man's expertise." Biddy squared her shoulders and caught her breath. "The man's passion for his work reflects in his fan following and the show's ratings, which are going to tank. And by the way, the posts about our episode are getting way more action than any previous episode."

"But we have no desire to be associated with this show ever again." I spun around to leave, then glared over my shoulder. "Unless, of course, it's at Dalwade Castle."

We stuck our noses triumphantly in the air and marched out.

Seventeen

WE HOPPED into my car and headed straight to Kilcarrigy. I was fired up after our confrontation or rather *presentation* to the show's producer, who'd barely gotten a word in during our rant. We needed to stop at the estate and give Kiernan a heads-up about our visit to the set. Not having heard from him, I assumed he wasn't aware of it.

"I untagged myself from the post, but even if she convinces the eejit to remove our names, it's out there, already viewed by thousands if not millions," Biddy said. "Here we are telling that producer to work this chaos to the show's advantage, when that's what we need to be doing."

I nodded, now in a more rational frame of mind. "We need to tell what really happened. How we uncovered Skelly. There are reporters, ghost-tour guides, tons of people wanting to hear our story."

"Ghost-tour guides? How brill is that?" Biddy's eyes lit with inspiration. "Maybe we could be on that ghost hunter's reality show. Maybe Kiernan would allow us to talk about the estate's ghost. That Skelly was messing with the filming because he was no longer buried and trying to get our attention."

"We'll figure all that out later. We definitely need to take advantage of our popularity. Make that jerk, and not us, look like the idiot for spreading lies. Ideally, I'd like Kiernan's approval. Yet it's not like I'd disclose any of my discoveries about his family or put him in a negative light. This would be a good thing for him as well."

On the way to town, I drove past the nursing home and then made a U-turn. Winnie had left two more voicemail messages.

"We've been bugging the woman to call us with information, and when she does, I put her on ignore status. That's not right. I owe her the courtesy to at least hear what she has to say."

Five minutes later inside Winnie's room, the woman fidgeted with the silver St. Brigid's cross resting against her chest. "After having mentioned our man's wool socks the other day, it reminded me of his toes."

Eeewwww. My nose crinkled. Biddy's top lip curled back.

"Can't believe I'd be forgetting about his socks. I always darned the farmhands' wool socks. The fella would joke that only one sock in a pair needed much darning. He was missing a big toe. That sock rarely wore out except for the heel. Not sure if this will be of help. If the toes even remained..." She grimaced, clutching the cross.

I'd been too shocked upon discovering a skeleton on my foot to have counted its toes.

I placed a hand gently on the woman's knee. "I'm sorry. I'm sure this is difficult."

She nodded. "Might you be able to pass this information on to the garda for me? Don't feel up to it."

Biddy smiled. "No worries. Of course we can be doing that."

I nodded. "If Garda Higgins doesn't know the details, he can check with the pathologist."

The timing of Farmhand Kerry's disappearance was likely a coincidence, unless my theory about him possibly having been a collector for Oscar's loan shark business was correct. It felt like I was working too hard at trying to connect something that wasn't connected. However, I wasn't breaking two promises in twenty-four hours. Besides, passing along the information on the woman's behalf wasn't actively reopening my investigation, as I'd promised Kiernan I wouldn't.

We entered the police station, and Garda Higgins greeted us with a faint smile. He rubbed his white beard while I recounted Winnie's story and inquired about the skeleton possibly missing a toe.

"Detective Inspector Cohan from Dublin won't be investigating the case. This will be announced later today. Case closed."

"Can you at least call the pathologist to verify if the skeleton is missing a toe?" I asked.

He shook his head, gesturing to a tall stack of papers on his desk. "I'll be adding it to the many crazy theories I've received."

"A missing toe isn't crazy," I said. "If it's missing, then the

case is solved. Once locals learn the garda don't plan to identify the victim, they're going to be flooding your office
demanding to know why and think you let them down.
Wouldn't you rather be a hero than a quitter?"

"Hometown hero, Garda's glory..." Biddy framed the air
with her hands. "I can see the social media hashtags now."

The man raised an intrigued brow.

"One toe, one call," I said. "Easier than us having to drive
to Dublin to ask the state pathologist ourselves."

"Actually," Biddy said, "it might not be a bad idea to
head to Dublin. While we're there, I could talk to one of the
forensic fellas about where my car is or if they've lost it.
Since the investigation is over, you certainly don't be
needing it."

Panic filled the officer's eyes. "I can be ringing the
pathologist."

Biddy gave the man a curious stare. "Why do you look
worried about me asking a forensic fella about my car?"

The man broke out in a sweat. His ruddy complexion
flushed a crimson color, and his breathing quickened.

"Janey!" Biddy's eyes widened. "Having a heart attack,
are ya?" Nurse Biddy darted around the counter, prepared to
administer CPR or other needed medical attention.

The man held up his hand, taking a step back from
Biddy, appearing off balance. "I'm grand."

"You don't be looking grand."

I joined Biddy, and we assisted the officer to his chair. I
snatched a book from his desk and fanned him while Biddy
insisted on taking his pulse.

The man shook his head. "I'm fine, except..." He
collapsed against his chair. "I know where your car is."

Biddy's head snapped back in surprise. "What does my car have to be doing with you nearly fainting?"

The officer heaved a deep sigh. "Because I have the yoke."

Biddy blinked in confusion. "It's not outside."

"It's in my drive, at home."

Biddy remained surprisingly calm, her professional bedside manner kicking in. "Why is my car at your place?"

The man grabbed tissues from a box on his desk and patted the sweat from his forehead. "Several months ago my wife lost her job. When we couldn't be making payments, we also lost her car. A few days ago her mum suddenly took ill. I couldn't be leaving the station, so I had her take your car to rush her mum to the A and E. I'd planned to have ya collect it that afternoon you came in, but her mum took a turn for the worse and my wife didn't want to be leaving the hospital. Thought I could be blaming the mess up on the forensic fellas." He shook his head. "Sorry. Was quite bold of me. Wasn't thinking straight."

Biddy stared at him in disbelief, at a loss for words.

He frowned, peering down at his desk. "Don't know what we'll be doing when I lose my job as well."

"Why will you be losing your job?" Biddy demanded.

He glanced up at her. "Once the sergeant learns what I did, he'll—"

"Would be a bit mad of you to be telling him what happened if he'd sack ya for it. As if you can be affording to be out of work."

The man's face lit with gratitude. "I'll have my wife be bringing the car by straightaway. She's at the hospital in Mullingar, so will be taking her just a bit."

"I'll pick it up tonight." Biddy gestured to the phone on

his desk. "Right now we have more important matters. We need you to be checking on the missing toe."

He smiled and snatched up the phone. While he was on hold, Biddy drummed her fingers impatiently against his desk and I tapped my foot against the tile floor. The pathologist finally came on the line and provided an immediate answer.

He hung up the phone. "Fella's missing a toe."

Biddy and I gasped. Shocked, confused, and relieved that Skelly was Farmhand Kerry, not Oscar. That meant Oscar was likely the killer and Ernest wasn't guilty.

"I'll call in on the woman and take her statement."

We sprang from our chairs.

"Ah, you can't be sitting in on our discussion."

"We'll be on standby to comfort her afterward," I said. "I'm sure this will be quite upsetting."

The officer gave Biddy an appreciative smile. "If you ever be needing anything, you can be calling on me."

With our luck, we'd be calling in the favor sooner than he'd imagined.

He locked up the station and left for the nursing home.

"That was awfully nice of you," I told Biddy as we headed to my car.

She shrugged. "Couldn't have the fella getting sacked before this case is solved." She smiled, looking pleased with herself, as she should. "What about the penny? Had it slipped through a hole in Oscar's pocket when he was burying the guy?"

"Maybe he'd tossed it in with the body hoping it would bring him good luck and keep him from getting caught. Based on the donations Dunphy's grocer made to the church, he was likely a religious man. Perhaps he thought it might bring him forgiveness. Besides the penny, Oscar clearly had dodgy dealings with the farmhand, among many others."

"So how was Suitcase Salesman and the break-in connected to the man's death if Farmhand Kerry disappeared months before?"

I shrugged. "Maybe the salesman found out about the murder and confronted Oscar. Oscar paid him to leave town immediately, which didn't leave him time to pick up his suitcase. We'll never know what actually happened. Just need to be happy we identified Oscar as the killer, and we identified the victim, or at least know his background and that he was from Kerry."

I didn't like unanswered questions. However, we'd cleared Kiernan's grandmother of having committed a horrific crime and his mentor from being involved with the murder. Preserving Kiernan's fond memories of loved ones and getting his life back on track was what mattered.

And hopefully this would help get my life back in order.

※   ※

While waiting for the garda to take Winnie's statement, we stopped in to visit Julia. Neither Elvis nor Julia greeted us at the woman's coconut-scented room. She was sitting in silence, staring out the window.

I rapped on the open door, and Julia turned to us, concern wrinkling her forehead. "I just heard the garda is in Winnie Sheehan's room. Hope she's okay."

I nodded, entering. "She's just discussing a matter with him." Wait a sec. "I'm sorry—did you just call her Winnie *Sheehan*? Thought her last name was *Dwyer*?"

Julia let out a faint laugh. "Fifty years later I still sometimes call her by her maiden name. Knew her as Winnie Sheehan when we attended school together. Can't believe Sheehan just popped into my head."

Luckily, it had since the name rang a bell.

"Was she by chance related to James Sheehan?"

The rasher and pork supplier who'd filed charges against Oscar and then gotten in a brawl with him because Oscar had cut off his livelihood.

"He was her father. Surprised a young lass such as yourself would have known the man. He died many years back."

"Read about him in an old paper." I glanced over at Biddy. "We should see how Winnie's doing."

Before leaving, Julia insisted we slather coconut-scented lotion on our hands. The bottle was already a quarter empty. Would have to pick her up another one.

Once out in the hallway, I grabbed Biddy's arm and propelled her toward the entrance rather than Winnie's room. We flew out the front door and into the parking lot. I reminded Biddy of James Sheehan's connection to Oscar Dunphy.

"Janey," she muttered. "Winnie made it sound like Oscar was just grand, giving kids free sweets and all. Why wouldn't she have mentioned her father's troubles with the dodgy man?"

I told Biddy about Oscar's loan shark ledger.

"Right, then." Biddy looked baffled. "Was she afraid if she brought up her father's troubles with Oscar, she'd be raising suspicions that *he'd* killed *Oscar*, instead of *Oscar* having killed *Farmhand Kerry*?"

"Yet if her dad killed *Oscar*, how does Winnie know that Oscar had a missing toe?"

"This can't be a coincidence, can it?"

Garda Higgins exited the building. He couldn't discuss the details of his conversation with Winnie except to acknowledge that she'd confirmed our story. We headed inside to discuss a different variation of the woman's story.

Winnie sat on her bed, clutching the St. Brigid's cross around her neck, her hand trembling. She was awfully upset about the death of a farmhand seventy years ago, whose name she hadn't even known.

Biddy and I pulled up chairs across from her.

"I'm glad it's finally over," Winnie said. "After all these years it's been proven that our man was the victim of foul play."

Biddy and I exchanged skeptical glances.

Biddy gestured to the woman's necklace. "That's a lovely cross. It's done a fab job protecting you all these years, seeing as you've lived a long life. Legend has it that besides protective powers, the cross brings one peace."

Winnie nodded, a tear slipping down her cheek.

Biddy wore a sympathetic expression. "It hasn't brought you peace, has it?"

The woman shook her head. "Nothing will except the truth." She choked back a sob.

Biddy sat on one side of Winnie, I sat on the other. I placed a comforting hand on her arm.

"The farmhand was a lie," she said. "It was Oscar Dunphy's remains buried there. I knew the man was missing a toe because his shoe and sock slipped off when I was dragging his body down the stairs."

Biddy and I gasped in shocked disbelief.

"Janey," Biddy muttered. "You killed the fella and buried him by yourself?"

"His mother helped me."

Oscar's mother helped drag her son's body down the same steps Kiernan freaked out about if someone got mud on them?

"It was actually her idea. I never should have agreed to it, but I hadn't much choice, seeing as I'd killed him." She clutched her necklace.

"Was it because of your father and his business dealings with Oscar?" I asked.

Anger sharpened the woman's soft features, and she pressed her glossed lips into a thin line. "The man ruined my family. My father lost the farm when I was in school. It destroyed my parents' marriage. He died at not even forty years old, leaving my mum to raise me and my younger brothers. My father never even met my children, his grand-children."

Biddy slipped an arm around the woman's shoulders. "You're going to be grand."

"'Twas an accident. I went there to beg him to not press charges against my husband, who was set on revenge for what Oscar had done to my family. Henri demanded money to keep quiet over the man's unfair and shady dealings. The Dunphys were a powerful family. I was afraid of what he might do to my husband." She nibbled on a purple finger-nail. "The horrible man made advances toward me. I pushed him away, and he fell against the brick fireplace. His mum heard the commotion and came running into the room. She stared in shock at her son lying dead on the floor. Rather than breaking down crying or threatening to ring the garda, she said her son had gotten what he deserved."

"That seems brutal," Biddy said.

"Before her husband's death, she'd discovered her son was swindling many of the locals. Raging, she'd told her husband about it. Turned out he'd already known yet hadn't done a thing to stop it. To make matters worse, he went against her wishes, leaving the house to Oscar once she was gone. She felt Ernest was the lad most deserving of the estate as well as the business."

"Where did you bury him?" I asked.

The garden shed wasn't public knowledge, so I wanted to confirm she was aware of the detail. It seemed crazy that people confessed to crimes they didn't commit. However, Ian had falsely confessed to his brother's murder, certain he was protecting his lover, Rhona. I wanted to make sure Winnie wasn't protecting someone.

"Under the gardening shed. With the help of a man."

"A salesman for the grocery store?" I asked.

She shrugged. "Haven't a clue. He had some sort of dealings with the Dunphys. He stopped by in the middle of it all. Not only did he offer to keep quiet but also to assist us with burying the body if Mrs. Dunphy made it worth his while. She paid him a load of quid to leave town without seeing a soul and to never return."

Precisely why he hadn't taken time to get his suitcase.

Biddy wore a puzzled expression. "What did the store's break-in have to do with this if Oscar's death happened at his house?"

"Mrs. Dunphy and I staged the break-in. She thought that claiming her son was attacked during a robbery would lead to fewer questions and people wouldn't be so suspicious."

"And nobody ever questioned Oscar's disappearance?" I asked.

"Not like the nasty bloke had a wife or friends. He and his brother, Ernest, didn't get on, so he believed his mother that Oscar wanted nothing further to do with the family and was starting a new life in Dublin."

It was amazing what people got away with before the internet. Two fabricated life stories in one family. Maybe I wasn't the only secret in my family's closet.

"Did you be telling anyone what happened?" Biddy asked.

"Merely Henri. Had to tell him. My dream had always been to marry and raise a family here. After all that, I couldn't stay here and live with what I'd done. We only returned to the area twenty years back."

Life was strange. Julia had dreamed of moving to Dublin with her friend Annie, but she ended up staying in Kilcarrigy. Whereas unfortunate circumstances had forced poor Winnie to give up her dream of raising a family in her small home-town and instead live in Dublin.

"It was self-defense and over seventy years ago," I said. "The guards surely won't pursue charges."

I hated to have to tell them. But how could I tell Kiernan the truth without telling the police?

And despite the horrible situation and the fact that Oscar had been a nasty human being, I felt an obligation to Skelly. I'd grown quite fond of Skelly...though not Oscar.

Eighteen

GARDA HIGGINS CAME STRAIGHT OVER to the nursing home and took Winnie's confession. Ultimately, it was the detective inspector's decision on how to proceed. Garda Higgins believed the case would be closed—ruled as self-defense and not intentional homicide. He promised to do everything he could to keep Winnie's name from being disclosed to the public. Why ruin the last few years of the poor woman's life?

He agreed to allow Biddy and me to tell Kiernan the story in person before he visited the estate and shared Skelly's identity. Kiernan would be relieved that Ernest's name had been cleared as both the killer and victim. Even though I'd pursued the investigation after having promised not to, all had turned out well in the end.

"It's better Oscar having been the victim rather than the killer," Biddy said.

I nodded. "If Ernest ever discovered the truth, I'm sure it was years later, and he never shared it with Kiernan's grandma Isobel."

"That's the story we're sticking with."

That Ernest had raced after the inn's owner to retrieve the salesman's suitcase could have been at his mother's request, not because *he'd* wanted to destroy evidence.

Thankfully, it hadn't rained much since Storm Skelly, so the estate's drive had dried up. No more pushing cars out of mud ruts. The crime scene tape was gone. The sun was shining. But I feared a dark cloud still loomed inside the house, and inside Kiernan Moffat.

Surprisingly, the appraiser answered the door with a smile, well-groomed hair, clean-shaven face, and crisply pressed tan slacks and a white button-up oxford. He ushered us inside, where a green shag rug replaced the Turkish one.

"Please excuse the hideous rug. Brought it down from a bedroom. Merely a temporary replacement while the other is being professionally cleaned."

He led us up the spotless wooden steps. I envisioned Winnie and Oscar's mom having dragged the man's body down the stairs and his shoe and sock slipping off to reveal his missing toe. A shiver crawled over me. When sharing Winnie's story with Kiernan, it probably wasn't a good idea to mention specifics as to how the two women had hauled the body to the shed.

The library's open red drapes welcomed us with sunshine and the aroma of freshly brewed tea mingled with a vanilla-scented candle covering up the stench of cigar smoke.

"Fancy a spot of tea?" Kiernan asked.

Biddy and I nodded, sitting on the brown leather sofa while he prepared our beverages. He placed a silver tray with tea service for two on the cocktail table in front of the sofa.

He relaxed in a brown wingback chair across from us with a teacup.

"I, er, have something to tell you?" I said, finally finding my voice.

He nodded. "Yes, I know."

Argh. Garda Higgins had promised to let us tell him.

"Ah, yes, the show's producer, Camille, rang and told me about your visit to the set."

Based on his calm demeanor, his call with the producer had gone well. Or he was merely happy to have closure and to move on to his next venture.

"That appraiser fella you mentioned is a total eejit," Biddy said.

He smiled at Biddy. "Yes, I heard you succeeded at putting the gobshite in his proper place. As you did Camille."

"Sorry if our visit caused you any problems," I said.

"On the contrary. Camille was quite humbled by it and has changed her tune. Reality set in, and she no longer fancies the idea of losing the show's top appraiser and having the ratings tank."

"Ah, brilliant," Biddy said. "That's fab news."

He eased out a calm breath. "Right, then. I need to thank you both for having my back when others didn't. Even when it was no benefit to yourself to do so." He glanced at the window, a faint mist in his blue eyes, his cheeks flushing. "Don't believe anyone has ever done such a thing for me before."

If the man started crying, I hadn't a clue how I'd react.

He stood from his chair. Instead of wrapping us in a group hug, he went over and grabbed four books off the desk. He handed Biddy a blue cloth-covered book with a gilded peacock on the front.

"The first illustrated copy of *Pride and Prejudice* with a preface by George Saintsbury, illustrations by Hugh Thomson. Only two hundred and fifty copies were printed in 1894."

Biddy stared in awe at the book. "Janey," she muttered. "Will have to be getting one of those floor safes to keep the yoke in. It's bloody lovely. Much better than that *Doctor Zhivago*, written by Boris Pasternak."

Kiernan gave her a sharp nod. "Fair play to ya. I knew you could read."

She smiled. "Thanks a mil."

Not just for the gift, but also his confidence in her ability to read.

He handed me a three-volume set of pristine orange cloth-covered books with gold writing and a crown on the front. The spine read *Letters, Queen Victoria, 1837-1861*. My heart raced.

"The correspondence covers a fascinating period from the time Victoria ascended the throne until she lost her dear Prince Albert. Should make for an interesting read. First edition, of course."

The oldest book I owned was *The Poky Little Puppy* with a frayed spine, worn edges, and my name written in pen all over the inside cover.

"These are...incredible." I blinked back the tears blurring my vision. "Thank you." I hugged the books to my chest, breathing in the scent of vintage paper and cloth covers.

Kiernan cleared his throat. "You're welcome. Yet let's not get emotional, shall we?"

I was going to become even more emotional if he took the books back after what I was about to confess.

"Um, there's actually something else I have to tell you."

Biddy sprang to her feet. "That can wait. We must craic on. I'm late for...a date."

I gave her pant leg a solid tug.

She reluctantly dropped down onto the couch.

Kiernan sat across from us. I explained that I'd broken my promise not to pursue the investigation. However, I really hadn't since it was purely by chance, as usual, that we'd solved the case and correctly identified Skelly. His expression remained unreadable until I finished.

A relieved look washed over him. "Ernest wasn't involved in any manner?"

I shook my head. "He hadn't a clue. He and Oscar were estranged, and Ernest never had a desire to reconcile."

That was my guess anyway.

Moisture filled the appraiser's blue eyes. He peered back over at the chair by the window where he'd read Ernest's entire vintage book collection as a boy. "I shouldn't have cared so much about what other people thought. What matters is what *I* think and how *I* felt about the man. Thank you for ensuring his reputation and my fond memories remain intact."

I choked down a lump of emotion.

Biddy sniffled next to me.

"I agree that there's no need for mentioning this Winnie woman's name to the public," Kiernan said. "The news and social media will crucify the poor thing and make her remaining days sheer hell. I'll discuss the matter with the garda."

"Speaking of social media..." I filled the appraiser in on the viral photo of Biddy and me circulating on the internet, possibly the news by now. "We'd like to defend ourselves against this idiot's lies."

"And clear our reputation as skeleton scavengers and body snatchers," Biddy said.

"Standing up for yourselves is the bloody right thing to do. It's what I should have done from the start before things became such a mess. Who knew how wretched people would become?"

Biddy and I just needed to figure out how to turn the scandal in our favor without making matters even worse.

"Despite everything, suppose I should give Oscar a proper burial," Kiernan said. "Can't be putting him in the family plot, the way Ernest felt about his brother and after his mother's involvement with covering up her son's death."

"Have him cremated," I said. "Spread his ashes somewhere else on the estate instead of under that large oak tree."

Kiernan nodded.

The doorbell rang, echoing up the stairs and startling us.

Kiernan stood, adjusted his collar, smoothed a hand over his hair, and popped a piece of spearmint gum into his mouth. "Sorry. I have a meeting."

It was apparently an important one.

As he escorted us down the stairs, Biddy leaned in toward me. "We didn't have time to ask him about the castle's episode."

I shrugged. It'd have to wait.

He opened the door and greeted the show's producer with a smile. Her blond hair was pulled back in a twist. An emerald-green sheath dress and matching coat brightened the green in her eyes, as did her green eyeshadow and liner.

Hmm... Fancy meeting.

Rather than giving Biddy and me the evil eye, the woman smiled sweetly. "Nice to see you both. Guess I'll be seeing you again in April. That castle looks like a lovely location." She flashed Kiernan a flirty smile. "We'll have to take a quick trip over to check it out."

The man responded with a steamy gaze. "Indeed."

She peered at us. "I honestly haven't a clue who moved the medal. It wasn't me, and nobody has confessed. However, I admit it was me who gave your names to that Twitter fella. Wasn't doing it to be mean. Was merely trying to do my job and help a friend." She smiled at Kiernan.

Biddy and I thanked the appraiser again for the books and headed toward my car.

A mysterious glint sparkled in Biddy's eyes. "See, a ghost was responsible for the shenanigans. Oscar, I bet." Her smile widened. "Looks like the filming is on."

"Among other things, it appears." I glanced over my shoulder up at the library window.

We laughed, giving each other a high five.

Five months and we'd be off to film in Scotland!

Upon arriving home, I uncorked a bottle of red wine to celebrate our success and spark our creativity while brainstorming how to conduct our own damage control. Biddy had threatened Gaelic Gobshite, promising to hunt him down at his favorite hangouts in Galway if he didn't remove the slanderous hashtags from his viral post. We needed our photo to remain on his Twitter page since it was the reason why hundreds of people had reached out to me requesting interviews about Skelly. Currently, we were sifting through dozens of printed-out emails.

Biddy crumpled a sheet of paper in her hand. "We should grant an exclusive interview to this nasty reporter, then sabotage it. Make her look like a right gobshite after what she did to Kiernan."

I nodded. "Unfortunately, that wouldn't be the most beneficial for us and the castle."

"The ghost hunter's show is still my number one choice."

"I don't want to turn this whole thing back into a media circus about ghosts."

"Who do you think moved the medal?"

I shrugged.

"Exactly. We can't rule anyone or any*thing* out. It's not like we'd be disrespecting Skelly. And Oscar certainly hadn't respected anyone in his life." Biddy was on the edge of the couch cushion. "We could do an exclusive interview at Kiernan's estate in exchange for a video filmed at Dalwade Castle. Have you even watched one of these ghost hunter's YouTube videos?"

"No."

"Every one of them has millions of views and almost always goes viral. And the two fellas are fierce gorgeous. We could take them through the castle's cemetery and the underground passageway haunted by Euphemia. The exposure would be brill."

I warmed to the idea, when the doorbell rang.

Biddy applied light-pink lipstick. She slipped the ponytail band from her blond hair and fluffed it.

Collin was picking her up for dinner.

We answered the door to find him dressed in a sporty blue windbreaker and brown hiking boots without a scuff on them.

Biddy gave his coat's zipper a playful tug. "This yoke is lovely."

"Thanks a mil. Fancy the boots? Was thinking they'd be grand for our hike in Wicklow next weekend."

Biddy smiled and didn't appear freaked out by the idea of their weekend away. "Maybe I should at least be buying some better runners for the walk." The couple headed down the drive hand in hand, and Biddy glanced back at me. "We'll talk more on the ghost hunters tomorrow."

Collin's gaze narrowed. "Another dead body, is there?"

"Not yet," Biddy said. "But I'm sure there will be before long."

She was undoubtedly right. Hopefully, further mysteries held off long enough for me to solve Gretta's DNA mystery. The woman had texted me on my way home from the estate, and I was fairly certain I knew why. She was due here in the next half hour.

I gave my dad a quick call and shared the wonderful news about filming at Dalwade Castle. I asked him to keep it a secret until I could tell the others. I was torn. Ava should be my next phone call. Ava and Rhona had selected the hotel for the reunion and were the initial investors. They were the ones who'd gotten the rest of the family on board. However, Ian had emailed me about the spike in hotel bookings after I'd mentioned it on *Rags to Riches Roadshow*. I could email him before calling Ava. If he discovered I'd *called* Ava after having *emailed* him, would he find that weird? It couldn't be any weirder than attempting to carry on my first phone conversation with the man.

The doorbell rang.

Gretta was standing at the door, biting her lower lip and holding a small box. Her ancestry DNA test. Heart racing, I let her in.

"I'm so nervous, I haven't any spit," she said.

I nodded, suffering from dry mouth, though my palms were sweating. I went and fetched us glasses of water while Gretta paced the living room floor. She guzzled her water, and I pulled up her Ancestry.com account on my laptop and registered the DNA kit.

Gretta stared at the small plastic tube in her hand. "This spit could change my life forever."

I nodded. "Several lives."

"For the better. I can feel it." She took the plunge and produced the required amount of saliva.

I packaged up the test and gave her a reassuring smile, and she headed to the post.

Fingers crossed that two Christmases in a row wouldn't suck. That Gretta's, her grandchild's, and his father's families weren't torn apart. And that the father wasn't a married local.

I grabbed a small slip of blue paper from my desk and jotted down a wish for the fairies. I tugged on my wellies and trekked through the long grass to the lone ash tree at the far end of the backyard. I opened the tiny weathered red door with yellow bees at the base of the tree trunk and tucked the slip of paper into the hiding space.

Kiernan's situation reinforced that blood relations often didn't mean more to a person than non-blood ones. My bond with my dad and Biddy was much stronger than my relationship with my sisters. Still, as a genealogist, I'd always be driven by a strong curiosity to learn about my biological roots. I was fortunate I had the chance to do so with Ian. I hoped Gretta was as lucky.

Heart racing, I eased out a calming breath. I slipped my phone from my back pocket and hit Ian's number on speed dial.

A MAGS AND BIDDY GENEALOGY MYSTERY
BOOK SIX

COMING AUGUST 2022

Genealogy Tips & Quips
Learn About Ancestry Research

Genealogy Research Tips

The following two genealogy research articles are from my nonfiction book, *Genealogy Tips & Quips*. In 2018 I began writing a genealogy column for my monthly author newsletter about my personal research experiences. I was writing articles faster than I was publishing newsletters, so I decided to compile them into a book. *Genealogy Tips & Quips* includes fifty articles and two extensive case studies—one about how a paternal DNA test revealed my family's royal lineage, and my quest to uncover family secrets. I hope you find these tips helpful.

Playing a Genealogist Sleuth
INSPECTOR CLOUSEAU OR SHERLOCK HOLMES?

Sometimes I feel more like the bumbling Inspector Clouseau than the skilled Sherlock Holmes when conducting genealogical research. Yet if I spend enough time on Ancestry.com, I'll usually solve my genealogy mystery either by sheer luck or deductive reasoning. The following is an example of how tracing your ancestry line requires keeping an open mind while piecing together clues to solve the puzzle. It can also involve a bit of mental gymnastics, which might require giving this tip a second read.

When I started researching Richard Tubbs for a friend, I knew he was born c. 1851 in London. I located the Tubbs family in the 1861 and 1871 censuses, which confirmed Richard's approximate birthdate, his parents' names—Richard Sr. and Elizabeth—and the family's address.

I searched Ancestry.com for Richard Jr.'s or his younger sister Ann's baptismal or civil birth records, but came up empty. So I looked for his parents' marriage record. I found a Richard Fossey Tubbs and Elizabeth Hale married in 1857. Six years *after* Richard Jr. was supposedly born and three years *after* his sister's birth. I might have assumed I had the wrong couple. However, the address on the marriage record was next door to where the family had lived in the 1861 census. I now had the critical piece of information that would eventually help me piece together this mysterious family. The father's middle name was Fossey.

I used the father's full name to search for Richard Jr.'s 1851 birth record. I found a baptismal record for a Richard Hale. I recalled that my Richard's mother's maiden name was Hale. The record noted the parents as Elizabeth Hale and Richard "Fossey" Hale. Well, wasn't that interesting? Fossey being a very uncommon name, I believed I had the correct family. I put in their daughter's birth year with the last name Hale, and ta-da, a record now appeared for an Ann Jane Hale with parents Richard and Elizabeth. FYI, the children's civil birth records were also filed with the mother's maiden name, Hale.

Next, I searched for the family in the 1851 census and found Richard and Betsy "Fossey" living at the same address as the children's baptismal records. Now their *last* name was the father Richard's *middle* name. Over a six-year period, the family used *three* different surnames on church and government documents. The mother's maiden name, Hale. The father's middle name, Fossey, and his last name, Tubbs. Had they been hiding from the law? Perhaps, but I believe it was because the couple had two children born out of wedlock. Despite the family having lived at the same residence when two baptisms and their marriage occurred, these events were held at *three* different churches. A family changing churches (not their religion) while remaining at the same residence was uncommon.

Once the parents were married, all future census and vital records noted family members with the last name Tubbs. However, I have not yet located Richard Tubbs Jr.'s marriage record or his children's baptismal or birth records. Maybe Richard Jr.'s children were born prior to his marriage and he followed family tradition, giving them his wife's maiden name, Wright. And so the mystery continues . . .

Psst. Did You Hear About...

A NEWSPAPER'S GOSSIP COLUMN MIGHT HAVE SOME JUICY FAMILY DETAILS

Another breakthrough with my Coffey family came from my ancestor Margaret Coffey's obituary, which noted two women and their husbands from Iowa having attended the funeral. I located the couples' marriage records online and discovered the women's father's name was Michael Coffey. But how was Michael related to my ancestor Patrick Coffey? A brother, cousin, nephew, or coincidence?

I went to the Wisconsin Historical Society and obtained twenty-five rolls of microfilm for the local newspapers from that time period. I scrolled through the gossip columns until I came across a snippet about the Coffey boys traveling to Iowa to visit their "uncle" Michael. Yet knowing that newspapers sometimes printed incorrect information, I searched until I found another notice referencing their "uncle." Bingo.

If I hadn't found Margaret's obituary, the newspaper's gossip column would have been a great resource. It often mentioned people in town not only visiting the living but also those attending funerals. The column would include residents involved in accidents or those affected by epidemics and illnesses. It would also pay condolences to parents who'd lost a newborn or young child, helping you identify unknown family members.

On a happier note, engagement announcements provided married surnames for those hard-to-trace female ancestors. Also, well-wishes to someone relocating to another town or state for a new job helps genealogists track them down. So if people hadn't heard the latest "news" through the grapevine, they could read about it in the weekly gossip column. While I was growing up, our local paper had a gossip column until the early 1980s.

The *Boston Pilot* had an interesting personal column titled "Missing Friends." From October 1831 to October 1921, the newspaper printed almost forty-five thousand advertisements from people searching for lost friends and relatives who had emigrated from Ireland to the United States. These ads provided details of the missing emigrant's life, including the county and parish of the person's birth, when he left Ireland, the port of arrival in North America, family members' names, and more. These advertisements have been compiled into several volumes of books and can be found on sites such as Ancestry.com and Findmypast, www.findmypast.com. I could spend all day perusing these ads.

Here is an ad placed in 1847 by a person searching for a Flannery couple from Derreenmanus, County Mayo, home-land of my Flannerys. I haven't confirmed a connection, even though Richard was a family name, but I sure hope these relations found each other. You can often feel a person's sense of desperation to locate loved ones. This ad provides a lot of genealogical information. However, I've come across ones that have even more details, such as a physical description, enabling you to picture your ancestor.

Of RICHARD FLANNERY, and ELLEN, his wife, formerly of Derreenmanus, near Castlebar, Co. Mayo. When last heard from they were in Constableville, NY. Any information respecting them will be thankfully received by her brother and his brother-in-law, Patrick McDonnell, addressed to him in care of Mr. Peter Carney, Brookline, MA.

You can search numerous online newspapers at Ancestry.com and www.newspapers.com.

The Irish Genealogy Toolkit website provides information for Irish newspapers at www.irish-genealogy-toolkit.com/irish-newspaper-archives.html.

The following are two websites on using newspapers in your research and how to find articles online:

www.theancestorhunt.com/blog/the-5-best-free-sites-for-online-newspaper-research-for-genealogy

www.genealogybank.com/explore/newspapers/all

Author's Note

Thank you so much for reading *How to Trace a Cold Case*. If you enjoyed Mags and Biddy's adventures, I would greatly appreciate your taking the time to leave a review. Reviews encourage potential readers to give my stories a try, and I would love to hear your thoughts. My monthly newsletter features genealogy research advice, my latest news, and frequent giveaways. You can subscribe at www.elizawatson.com. Thanks a mil!

About Eliza Watson

When Eliza isn't traveling for her job as an event planner or tracing her ancestry roots through Ireland and Scotland, she is at home in Wisconsin working on her next novel. She enjoys bouncing ideas off her husband, Mark, and her cats, Frankie and Sammy.

Connect with Eliza Online

www.elizawatson.com
www.facebook.com/ElizaWatsonAuthor
www.instagram.com/elizawatsonauthor

Made in the USA
Middletown, DE
04 June 2022

66669879R00126